Jeremy caught a~~~~~ ~~~~~ sadness in her eyes as sh~~~~~ those words. Did this pretty woman in the flowing skirt and warm green sweater have problems, too?

He couldn't imagine that. Gabi's smile was too bright, her walk too proud. She obviously had a strong faith, since she taught Sunday school here at the church. But he supposed a lot of people put on a happy face over their worries, faithful or not. His parents had certainly been doing that for years. For all of his life.

"Thanks for helping me out. Maybe I'll see you in church."

Jeremy couldn't muster up another smile. "Maybe."

He watched as Gabriela Valencia disappeared into the room down the hall. And took all the light with her.

DAVIS LANDING:
Nothing is stronger than a family's love

LENORA WORTH

has written more than forty books for three different publishers. Her career with Love Inspired Books spans close to fourteen years. Her very first Love Inspired title, *The Wedding Quilt*, won *Affaire de Coeur*'s Best Inspirational for 1997, and *Logan's Child* won an *RT Book Reviews* Best Love Inspired for 1998. With millions of books in print, Lenora continues to write for the Love Inspired and Love Inspired Suspense lines. Lenora also wrote a weekly opinion column for the local paper and worked freelance for years with a local magazine. She has now turned to full-time fiction writing and enjoying adventures with her retired husband, Don. Married for thirty-five years, they have two grown children. Lenora enjoys writing, reading and shopping... especially shoe shopping.

Christmas Homecoming
Lenora Worth

Love Inspired

Special thanks and acknowledgment to Lenora Worth for her contribution to the Davis Landing miniseries.

Recycling programs for this product may not exist in your area.

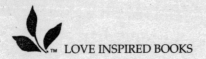

LOVE INSPIRED BOOKS

ISBN-13: 978-0-373-78691-6

CHRISTMAS HOMECOMING

Copyright © 2006 by Harlequin Books S.A.

www.LoveInspiredBooks.com

Printed in U.S.A.

I will lift up my eyes to the hills—from whence comes my help? My help comes from the Lord, Who made heaven and earth.
—*Psalms* 121:1–2

To anyone who has ever been away from home
at Christmas. I hope this story helps you
find your way back.

Chapter One

Swish. Swish. Swish. Jeremy Hamilton lifted the paint brush over his head, thinking his neck would be permanently damaged if he didn't get this room finished soon. The cream-colored paint refused to stick to the wall. Most of it was all over him—in his hair, on his old shirt and splattered across the aged, spotted drop cloth underneath the rickety ladder. Groaning out loud, he almost threw down the brush in defeat.

But Jeremy had never been a quitter.

Well, not until a few months ago, at least.

He stopped painting and held the dripping brush over the bucket perched precariously on the ladder, memories swirling through his mind just like the paint pooling under his soggy brush. Outside the wide double windows, a December wind howled and fussed, causing leftover fallen leaves to dance across the parking lot.

How had December come so quickly? And how had his life taken such a turn that even now, all these months later, he was still spinning in the wind just like those leaves?

With just a few words from his powerful father, Wallace Hamilton, Jeremy's whole life here in Davis Landing, Tennessee, had been turned upside-down. He'd gone from firstborn heir and vice president of a vast publishing conglomerate to being someone he didn't even know himself.

He wasn't really a Hamilton. His biological father, Paul Anderson, had died in a motorcycle accident before Jeremy was born, before his mother Nora could even tell her fiancé she was pregnant with his child. So for thirty-five years, Jeremy had been living a lie.

Worse, his parents, Wallace and Nora Hamilton, had also been living with that lie, even though they'd done their best to make a good life for their family. They'd worked hard to become pillars of the community, they'd been faithful to their church, and they'd done everything in their power to love and protect their six children, including him. Especially him, Jeremy reminded himself now.

Wallace Hamilton, once a wild playboy with a string of conquests, had fallen in love with delicate Nora McCarthy, and he'd married her knowing she was carrying another man's child. That endearing act and the devastating secret behind it had been the foundation of their marriage—a good, solid union in spite of its beginnings. But finding out the truth had rocked Jeremy's safe, secure world and shaken his own faith to its very foundations.

Wallace had been so ill with leukemia, and so unreasonable because of his helplessness, that he'd turned on Jeremy, taking out all his frustrations from his sickbed. *How long has he secretly resented me?* Jeremy wondered now, and not for the first time. That had been the burning question in Jeremy's mind since he'd learned the truth. How long had his adoptive father wanted to tell Jeremy that he shouldn't be a part of Hamilton Media? That he didn't really belong, after all?

Probably since the day I was born.

Which was why Jeremy had left Davis Landing a few months ago to do some soul-searching, and to find out more about his biological father's family. That long journey hadn't brought him any answers, just more questions and more doubts. So many doubts. His paternal grandparents down in Florida had welcomed him, but they'd obviously had mixed feelings regarding his existence. After all, they'd been estranged from their only son when he'd died. Jeremy felt the parallels of that clear truth as he now thought about his estranged relationship with Wallace.

Did he really want to stay away, knowing his father might not make it? He'd never forgive himself if that happened, and yet, he hadn't been able to go and see Wallace since coming home a few days ago.

Knowing that Paul Anderson had died away from his family made Jeremy feel petty and small. Especially after he'd tracked his grandparents down.

It had been an awkward reunion, but Jeremy was glad he'd made the effort. At least it had brought the Andersons some sort of comfort and closure. And maybe, a new beginning.

"You come back anytime," his grandmother Thelma had told Jeremy the morning he decided to leave Florida. She hugged him tight. "You don't know how much it means to me, to see you, to know I have a grandson. Your father…well, he was a rebel, a real handful. I wish I could have told him how much I loved him."

Jeremy had seen pictures. He looked just like Paul Anderson—dark-haired, blue-eyed, tall and angular. It must have been hard on his grandmother, seeing the image of her son in the flesh after all these years.

It seemed to be even harder on Chester Anderson. His grandfather had resented Jeremy, maybe because he'd been denied ever knowing he had a grandson. Chester had tried, but in the end, his silence and his condemnations of Thelma's quiet faith, had only caused the gap between Jeremy and him to widen.

"We'll go fishing next time," he'd said to Jeremy. "Maybe on a Sunday. I fish while Thelma does her church thing."

Jeremy had figured that was Chester's way of saying he'd like to see him again. And it had also been his ornery grandfather's way of telling Jeremy that he wasn't a believer like his wife.

So Jeremy had left, his doubt and his confusion

scattering out into the balmy Florida breezes. Not even a vast ocean had helped him find the answers he'd needed.

And here he stood, different but hoping to be the same. He'd come full circle, and yet he was still very lost. He'd come home to find all his siblings either getting married or falling in love. Hoping to find some strength in his family, Jeremy had discovered that he was as alone as ever. That feeling of isolation echoed through his mind over and over, causing him to stay away from his ailing father's bedside. He wasn't ready for another confrontation, and he certainly couldn't take any more revelations.

He could see now what he hadn't been able to pinpoint growing up—he'd always had a feeling of being set apart from his brothers and sisters, a feeling of somehow being different, of not quite measuring up. Maybe because he wasn't really their flesh and blood. He even looked different, more like his real father, based on the pictures his grandmother had shown him. He was the half brother. He had no claims to the Hamilton empire. Except those he felt deep inside his heart.

Alone, aloof and isolated, he'd come home, hoping to find solace with his family, but he'd never felt more lonely. He shouldn't have come back, and yet, he'd needed to do that very thing. In spite of his doubts and frustrations, the road, and maybe God's gentle voice, had brought Jeremy home.

He had to wonder at the irony of being here now, inside the Northside Community Church, since he hadn't been very faithful lately. Maybe the Lord was trying to remind Jeremy of his real roots right here in this church and this town. Roots that ran deeper than blood or birthrights.

"By allowing me to waste paint and ruin my favorite old shirt?" Jeremy asked, his hushed words echoing out over the empty room. "You sure do have a strange sense of humor, Lord."

Jeremy slapped paint onto the wall, thinking he wasn't being entirely fair in thinking the worst of his parents. Wallace had married Jeremy's mother, first to protect her, but mostly because he loved her. And Wallace still loved Nora. Jeremy knew this in his heart, but that fact didn't soften the feelings of betrayal and distrust he'd experienced the day Wallace had called Jeremy into his hospital room to tell him the truth. He could still hear his father's weak, harsh words.

You have no right, Jeremy. No right to go against my word on how things should be run at Hamilton Media. Do you understand me?

No, Dad, I'm afraid I don't understand.

Jeremy remembered his mother's pale face, her shaking hands. Her pleas. "Wallace, now is not the time—"

But Wallace had found the strength to come up off his pillows. "It's the perfect time. I might not make it, Nora. Things might change for good. And I won't have someone who isn't even my own blood ruining what I've worked so hard to build."

The shocked silence that had followed still

haunted Jeremy's mind, silence that stretched out with only the beeping of machines to keep it from seeming like a bad dream.

"What did you say?"

Wallace had looked stunned himself, then embarrassed, his eyes went to his wife's face. "I'm sorry, son. We should have told you years ago—"

"We only wanted to protect you," his mother had interrupted, tears in her eyes.

"Protect me from what, Mother? What's going on?"

"You're not my son," Wallace had blurted, his words turning into a wheezing cough.

Nora had urged her husband back on the pillows. "Your biological father was a man named Paul Anderson. He died in a motorcycle accident, before I could—" She glanced at Wallace. "I was pregnant when your father—when Wallace married me."

You're not my son.

Those words had echoed over and over in Jeremy's mind, screaming to him until he'd lashed out at his parents. "How could you? How could you do this to me?"

The scene that had followed hadn't been Jeremy's finest hour. He'd told Wallace in no uncertain terms that he quit; he wouldn't work for a man who'd lied to him all his life.

Jeremy had walked out of the hospital and, other than a few short conversations with his siblings and his mother, hadn't made any effort to be a part of the Hamilton family since. Until Thanksgiving.

The holiday traditions had pulled at him, bringing him home.

Now, as he stood painting over the old, battered wall of the daycare room, Jeremy couldn't help but feel as if he were painting over all the flaws in his own life, too. Maybe there was something to be said for a fresh canvas.

"You know, the paint is actually supposed to go on the *wall*."

Jeremy turned at the soft, feminine tone, and managed to sling paint out in an arc all over his blue broadcloth shirt. Holding the dripping paintbrush, he smiled sheepishly. His smile felt strained and out of practice, but he tried to keep his voice light. "Really?"

The woman stepped into the room, careful to avoid the corner where Jeremy was working, her dark eyes inquisitive and full of mirth. "Really."

"I'll keep that in mind," he said as he slowly lowered the brush over the bucket. Then he waved a hand toward the wall. "Does it look that bad?"

She gazed up, looking around the room. "No, it actually looks pretty good, considering all the crayon marks and dents and pings we've had to endure. We're going to paint a mural of Noah's Ark over most of it anyway, so I think it'll be just fine."

Jeremy held up his hands. "I'm certainly not going to sign up for *that* particular job, so don't even ask."

She laughed at that, the sound as soft as a melody. "I heard you talking to yourself," she said, advancing another step. "Thought you might need some company."

Jeremy grinned, some of the tension leaving his body. "Thanks, I think. That makes me feel much better about things. I'm sorry. I hope I didn't disturb you with my groans and rantings."

"Not at all. I just came by to gather some papers—I teach Sunday School here." Then she smiled again. "I heard all this noise, and thought maybe someone had unleashed an old bear in the nursery, so I came to inspect. I'm the nosy type."

Her vivid smile brought a ray of light into the open, airy room, immediately pushing away the winter chill. She was petite and olive-skinned with big hazel eyes and long brown hair that reminded Jeremy of an antique doll his sister Heather had received for Christmas long ago. He caught a whiff of a light, exotic scent that had somehow gotten past the paint fumes.

"I'm not a bear," he said, his hands braced on the ladder. "Just a frustrated artist, I think."

"I'm Gabriela Valencia," the woman said, her smile still intact as she stared up at him. "Gabi. And we do appreciate your efforts, believe me. We've been hoping to remodel this part of the building for months now. We need all the help we can get if we want to have it done by Christmas."

"Well, *Gabi*, I'm just a volunteer," Jeremy said, not ready to tell her who he really was, even though she had an expectant look on her pretty face. He didn't want to see her smile vanish just yet. And he figured it would the minute she heard his name.

"We like volunteers," she replied. "They work cheap."

He laughed at that, surprised that he remembered how to laugh. "It is kind of nice to be alone and busy. No clocks ticking, no deadlines to fight."

"You sound like a man who speaks from experience."

He looked out the window. The sky looked gray and cold. "You could say that."

He didn't want to elaborate. He'd reluctantly agreed to help out here at the insistence of Dawn Leroux. The woman who'd once been his brother Tim's administrative assistant was now the woman Tim loved and planned to marry. She could be very persuasive when she set her mind on something. No wonder Tim had fallen so hard for her.

And no wonder Tim seemed more mellow and relaxed. His brother was in love…and happy. Jeremy envied that, and he was going to try very hard to mend fences, not tear down his brother's newfound contentment.

When Jeremy had arrived home just in time for Thanksgiving dinner at the Hamilton estate, he'd been surprised by two things. First, his brother Tim had apologized to Jeremy and welcomed him back home and back to Hamilton Media, when he was ready. And second, Tim introduced Jeremy to his fiancée, Dawn Leroux, and explained that because of Dawn, he was now a changed man. After some quiet conversation around the fireplace later, Dawn had gently suggested Jeremy might enjoy doing some volunteer work at the church to get his mind off his problems.

Painting had certainly done that, he thought now as he gave up and came down off the ladder, his manners kicking in, in spite of his discomfort at being here. "I'm kind of new to this type of work."

"I can see that," the woman said, circling the long room with a critical eye. She pointed to the wall he'd just finished. "You missed a spot there."

Jeremy looked up, then laughed. "Or two. I guess it's true you get what you pay for. I painted the ceiling, too, but I think I got most of the paint on me and the drop cloth."

She nodded. "It'll turn out just fine, I think. This old building has seen a lot of children come and go, my two girls included. We want to give it a fresh start for all the other babies we hope to bring into the church."

"A fresh start." Jeremy wiped his hands on an old rag. "I like the sound of that."

"Would you like something to drink?" she asked as she started toward the door. "We have some coffee in the office and there might even be a pastry from Betty's left in the break room."

Jeremy closed his eyes for just a minute. "Ah, Betty's Bake Shoppe and Bookstore. Fuel and knowledge all in one place—what an unbeatable combination."

"You've eaten there?"

He liked the slightly accented sound of her question. And he really liked the beautiful flash of fire in her eyes.

"Many times," he said, not bothering to explain. "But I don't need anything, thanks." Then, since he wasn't quite comfortable being back home, let alone working at the church, he looked at his watch and started putting his brushes in the soak bucket in the corner. "I have to go. I'll clean up here and try to hide the mess I made."

She looked confused and a bit disappointed. "I didn't mean to interrupt—"

Jeremy regretted being so standoffish, but he was still uneasy with his new identity, or lack thereof. "No, no. It's just that I only had a couple of hours and I've already worked past my time here. I'll be back to finish the job, I promise."

"Okay, then." She pointed to his hair. "You… uh…have a big glob of paint right in the middle of your head."

Jeremy reached up to rub his fingers over the sticky matted spot of cream in his dark hair. "I don't think I'll give up my regular job just yet." *Whatever that job might be.*

"Turpentine," she said, nodding. "It smells terrible, but it'll take the paint out. Just be careful, or you might wind up with a bald spot."

"Right." Jeremy wondered how such a dainty little woman could possibly know anything about remodeling and repair. But then, she obviously was a *married* woman. She'd mentioned two kids. Probably helped her husband around the house on week-ends. That image brought Jeremy a pang of regret, to be quickly replaced with a resolved indifference. "I'll have to get a shower before I go—"

He'd almost said *before I go to Hamilton Media*, but Jeremy remembered he didn't really have a place there anymore, in spite of his brother Tim's efforts to bring him back into the family business. "Before I go to work," he finished, uncomfortable with the way her big eyes watched him.

"You must keep long hours," she said as she led the way out the door. "It's close to five now."

"I have odd hours, true," he replied. And lately, those hours had tumbled over each other with a never ending frequency that seemed as long and winding as the nearby Cumberland River.

She tossed her long brown hair over her shoulder as she headed back down the church hallway. "Tell me about it," she said turning to give him a direct gaze. "Isn't life always tough for the working man, or in my case, the working woman?"

Jeremy caught a hint of some deep sadness in her eyes as she voiced those words. Did this pretty woman in the flowing skirt and warm green sweater have problems, too?

He couldn't imagine that. Her smile was too bright and sure, her walk too proud and precise. She obviously had a strong faith, since she taught Sunday School here at the church. But he supposed a lot of people put on a happy face over their worries, faithful or not. His parents had certainly been doing that for years. For all his life.

She lowered her head, looking shy for just a minute. "Thanks for helping out. Maybe I'll see you in church."

Jeremy held her gaze, but he couldn't muster up another smile. "Maybe."

He watched as Gabriela Valencia disappeared into the room down the hall. And took all the light with her.

He never told me his name.

Gabi hurried inside the house, intent on getting the girls a quick supper while they finished their homework. As she opened the door, she was bombarded by voices and barks and the blare of the television, all coming at her at once.

"Mommy, can Lauren spend the night with us Friday?" This came from her youngest, Talia. The eight-year-old jumped and bounced around as Gabi dropped her groceries on the tiny kitchen counter.

"I told her it's *my* turn to have a friend over," Veronica, her oldest, ten and going on twenty, said before Gabi could take a breath. Pushing her younger sister out of the way, Veronica stomped her purple-sequined sneakers on the tile floor. "It's *my* turn, Mommy."

"I can't sit with the girls tomorrow, Aunt Gabi. I have to stay after school and work on a project for my English class."

Gabi turned, almost tripping over the barking

mutt they'd picked from one of her brother Arturo's many litters. "Down, Tramp. I'll get you a treat in just a minute." Letting out a long sigh, she stared at her sixteen-year-old niece, Sonia, oldest child of her brother Juan Carlos. "That's okay, Sonia. I'll just have to ask Mama to come sit with the girls tomorrow."

"Are you sure?" Sonia asked, heading out the door. "I have to do this project to bring my grade up."

"Not a problem," Gabi responded. "School comes first, even if it means these two have to occasionally get spoiled by their grandmother."

Sonia grinned, then left to walk the short distance to her own house. "See you later."

"Yes," Talia said, pumping her little fist. "Maybe Nana will help me make cookies for my class party."

"I'm sure she'd love to do that, honey," Gabi said as she put away milk and eggs, ignoring Talia's obvious frustration that Gabi hadn't had time to help with cookies at the last class party. "And about this weekend, Talia, let's let Roni have a friend over Friday, since she and her friends stay up later. You can have someone over Saturday night—and take your friend to church with us Sunday, okay?"

The girls eyed each other, each trying to decide who'd gotten the better deal.

"I can live with that," Veronica, or Roni as everyone called her, said, nodding her head. Her long brown ponytail bobbed as she strolled away, her whole stance reminding Gabi of the girls' deceased father, Octavio.

"Works for me," Talia said, launching her tiny body against Gabi's skirt. "I'm glad you're home, Mommy."

"Me, too, baby," Gabi said, her thoughts still on the handsome stranger she'd found painting the daycare room at church. "Now do me a big favor and turn off that television. You need to finish your school work before you watch any more TV."

Talia mumbled her protest, but did as Gabi asked, while Gabi went back to thinking about the man she'd met today.

He sure did fit the role of the strong, silent type. Not too forthcoming with details. Good-looking and surely a gentleman. It wasn't so much his clothes—even though they'd been old and paint-covered she could tell they'd probably cost a pretty penny new. It was the way he carried himself, the way he smiled, or tried *not* to smile. He seemed like a man who could be comfortable in any setting, even a church nursery. *Could be.* At first, he'd seemed unsure, until she'd made him laugh. And what a nice laugh he had, a little rusty and throaty, but very enticing.

Stop it, she told herself as she opened a can of vegetable soup, then dug inside the refrigerator to find cheese for grilled cheese sandwiches.

But Gabi had always been too curious for her own good. She'd always been able to single out wounded souls, according to her mother, Marisol Marquez.

"You have a gift for helping others, Gabi," her mother used to tell her. "A nurturing soul."

Well, that nurturing soul hadn't helped her save her own husband, Gabi thought now. Which was why she'd made a solemn vow since his death to put her children first. Love wasn't in her future, except for the love she felt for her girls, and the love she felt for God's enduring salvation. She was a working mother and a widow who'd soon turn thirty. She had a steady job in administration at Community General and she had a good solid group of friends at church. She mostly met herself coming and going— no room for romance in her busy life.

And yet, as she sat down to say grace with her girls, Gabi couldn't help but think of the interesting, quiet stranger she'd met that afternoon. He should have looked so out of place standing there, all splattered in paint.

But to Gabi, he'd looked just right for some reason.

She'd have to call her best friend Dawn and give her the lowdown. Just for fun. Just for some girl talk. After all, it had been a very long time since Gabi had felt like talking about a man.

Maybe too long.

Chapter Two

A chilly wind whipped at Gabi's wool overcoat as she hurried the girls toward the sanctuary of the Northside Community Church. "C'mon, we don't want to be late for the service."

The century-old white-brick church located across the river from Davis Landing in Hickory Mills was all abuzz this morning as the faithful filed out of the education buildings tucked behind the sanctuary, headed to hear one of Reverend Charles David Abernathy's rip-roaring sermons.

The big, redheaded preacher could be as blustery as this wind, but he had a heart of gold and he loved each and every one of his parishioners. That membership included both the affluent people from Davis Landing and the average working families here in Hickory Mills, where Gabi lived.

"I'm cold," Talia whined, pulling her pink down jacket over her pleated plaid skirt.

"Well, the sooner we get inside, the warmer you will be," Gabi pointed out, a strand of dark hair blowing across her face. "Roni, hurry up," she said over her shoulder, her hand coming up to pull the escaping strand back from her jawline.

Veronica was giggling and whispering to her older friend Samantha Hart. No telling what those two were cooking up. But Gabi was glad her girls had such good role models as the Hart family. She knew her children were always safe and well taken care of when they were with Angela and Dave and their girls.

Gabi made it up the steps, then turned one more time to call out to her lagging older child. "Roni—"

She stopped, her heart picking up its pace as she saw him. Gabi took a second glance, just to make sure. It was him all right. The man she'd talked to two days ago in the daycare room of the church. He'd just gotten out of an expensive sedan, and he was walking up to the church with some of the Hamilton clan.

He sure cleans up nicely, Gabi thought as she took in the tall man dressed in a tailored overcoat and dark wool suit. His outfit probably cost more than one of her weekly paychecks, Gabi decided, wondering who this man really was.

He looked up then, his eyes locking with hers. At first, he seemed apprehensive and unsure, but then he sent her a hesitant smile, and he kept looking until Gabi felt a tug on her coat.

"Mom?"

Gabi glanced down at Talia. "What, honey?"

"Inside, remember? You wanted to get inside."

"Right, so I did." Gabi dropped her gaze, then turned to find her friend Dawn Leroux coming toward her.

"Dawn, hi! I tried to call you the other night. I wanted to talk to you about *him*. Only I didn't know that he was...well, *him,* then." She lifted her head toward the stranger. "You weren't home."

And now she wished she'd left a message. But Gabi had decided then that Dawn's not being home had to be a sign to drop the whole thing. She had no business asking questions about a handsome stranger, especially since the stranger was obviously a friend of the Hamiltons. And way out of her league.

Dawn glanced in the direction of Gabi's gaze. "Oh, *him.* I wanted to talk to you about him, too," Dawn said, her tone a bit too smug, her blue eyes bright with hope. "He does have a striking presence, doesn't he?" Then, as if realizing what Gabi had said, she asked, "What about him?"

"I've met him," Gabi whispered as they walked into church. "He was painting in the daycare the other day."

"Really? That's great," Dawn said, grinning. "I convinced him to help out. Oh, I'm so glad he actually took my advice."

Realization flared through Gabi. "*That's* the man you told me about—the man who left town because of a personal crisis?"

"That's him," Dawn said. "My future brother-in-law, Jeremy Hamilton."

Jeremy Hamilton. He seemed so different from all the rest. Of course, if the rumors were true—he *was* different.

They found a pew and both women sank down, the girls settling beside Gabi. Her mouth fell open as she turned to whisper to Dawn. "He's a Hamilton? You sure didn't mention that," she said, her gaze scanning the church doors for any sign of the topic of conversation.

Gabi quickly turned to face forward as Jeremy entered with his brother Tim. Suddenly all the pieces began to fall into place. This explained his almost aloof behavior the other day when she'd stumbled upon him painting. The man had every reason to be aloof. The Hamiltons were the local dynasty in these parts. Upper crust and top shelf. She couldn't believe she hadn't at least recognized him that day. But she'd never mingled in the same social circles as Jeremy Hamilton.

"I can't believe you didn't tell me," she whispered to Dawn.

Dawn glanced down at the church bulletin, then frowned. "But I did. I told you all about him."

Leaning close, Gabi replied, "You just said you had a friend who'd been going through a rough time and needed some space, so you suggested he volunteer at the church." Then she brought a hand to her mouth. "He's the older brother. The one who—"

Dawn interrupted with a whispered sigh. "He's still a Hamilton, no matter who his biological father was. And he's struggling, Gabi. With so many things. Jeremy and Tim have been at odds for a long time, but Tim wants to make amends. Jeremy is still hurting, though, and he needs to feel the love and trust of his church home. That's why I suggested he volunteer here."

Gabi lowered her head. It was so like gentle Dawn to figure out a way to put Jeremy at ease, and to bring him back to his faith. "I understand that, but you could have warned *me*. I actually flirted with the man!"

Dawn lifted an eyebrow, then smiled. "I didn't tell you his name because I didn't want to gossip in detail about his personal problems," she said, glancing back to wave to other church members. "And I didn't know he'd show up at the church so quickly." Then she grinned again. "And I certainly didn't plan on you running into him there, even though that worked out perfectly, if you ask me."

"What do you mean?" Gabi said, careful to keep her voice low. All around them, people were greeting each other and laughing and talking. It was always like this before the service began.

Dawn shot her another hopeful glance. "Oh, nothing. Just…well…he's lonely, Gabi. He needs a friend. And you're—"

"A single *mother*," Gabi reminded her, her eyes going wide as she emphasized that fact. "A single mother from the wrong side of the tracks. And he's the CEO of Hamilton Media. Dawn Leroux, are you trying to set me up with Jeremy Hamilton?"

"Maybe," Dawn replied. "And he's not the CEO

these days. But I'm hoping we can work on that, too." Then her smile widened as Tim Hamilton came up the aisle and sat down beside her.

Gabi spoke to Tim, then stared ahead, listening while Dawn and Tim whispered softly to each other, their newfound love endearing and sweet. Then she felt Dawn's arm on hers.

"Scoot over."

Gabi glanced up as she moved down to make room. She knew who it would be, waiting to take a seat at the end of the pew. Jeremy Hamilton looked at her, waved a hand, then sat down, his head turned toward her. He mouthed a "Hi, there," his eyes moving over Gabi and her girls.

Gabi gave him a weak smile, then turned to fuss over Talia and Roni as the organ music indicated the start of the service.

"Who is that, Mommy?" Roni asked, leaning forward to peer down the pew.

"Just a friend," Gabi said, pushing her inquisitive daughter back. "Don't stare, honey. It's impolite."

"Well, he keeps staring at *us*," Talia pointed out, waving at Jeremy.

He waved back. And finally cracked a smile.

"He's just being friendly," Gabi said. Then she handed her daughter crayons and a fresh sheet of notepaper from her purse. "Draw me a picture."

As the choir began singing the intro, Gabi stole another glance down the pew herself. Jeremy Hamilton was indeed smiling at her. And that smile sent a warm thrill all the way down to Gabi's black leather ankle boots.

Oh, Lord, she began to pray. *I'm sure in trouble here. Please help me to put this man out of my mind. Let me be a friend to him, to minister Your tender mercies, nothing more.*

But that particular prayer seemed to go unheard. Because all during the service, Jeremy Hamilton was front and center in Gabi's thoughts, and for more reasons than just tender mercies.

Jeremy was glad to be out of the old church. Slipping on his overcoat, he took a long breath of the frigid December air, his gaze scanning the sloping churchyard and the footbridge covering a gurgling creek that met up with the Cumberland River just beyond the trees. The familiar stained-glass windows, oak-paneled walls, and high-arched ceiling of the old sanctuary should have brought him some sort of comfort. Months ago, he'd prayed for his father in the tiny prayer room inside the church. He'd felt safe and secure there, having no doubt that God would take care of his father. And that God would take care of him, too.

Now, in spite of the familiar surroundings and all the smiles and greetings, he'd felt uncomfortable sitting there with everyone glancing at him. He wasn't so secure in his faith on this cold Sunday morning.

They all knew his shame. They all knew his pain. Thanks to someone leaking his true parentage to their rival paper the *Observer*, everyone in Davis

Landing knew that Wallace wasn't Jeremy's father. And while no one at church today had been unkind to him, Jeremy couldn't help but feel their intense scrutiny. He'd been away; he was estranged from his powerful, sick father. He and his brother Tim had been feuding and at odds. Jeremy wasn't at all surprised that the grapevines and gossip mills were going full throttle against him.

But Tim wants all of that to end, Jeremy reminded himself, still surprised that his high-maintenance younger brother had mellowed over the last few months. Maybe it was time for Jeremy to take some initiative and try to meet his brother halfway. Coming here today had been the first step, but now it seemed to be just one more bad decision.

Feeling determined after hearing Reverend Charles David's impassioned sermon about King David and how he'd overcome all his mistakes, Jeremy held his head up, taking in the crisp noon-time air. He'd go and visit his mother later, after he'd had some time to think. Right now, he only wanted to get away from the cluster of after-church minglers who seemed intent on laughing and talking their way out of the sanctuary.

Like David the shepherd crying out in the wilderness, Jeremy wanted to be alone with his torment. There were still so many things he needed to sort through—such as what he wanted to do with the rest of his life. He also wanted to contemplate who could be trying to destroy his family, since someone obviously continued to leak one scandal after another regarding the Hamiltons. The latest had involved his baby sister Melissa's out-of-wedlock pregnancy. Thank goodness Melissa now had Richard McNeil to love and protect her. She could probably use some kind words from her oldest brother, too, Jeremy thought. He hadn't been very kind to anyone lately.

Glancing around, he looked for Tim to tell his brother he was leaving. In spite of his tentative truce with his brother, and his mother Nora's pleas for him to forgive and forget, he wouldn't be attending Sunday dinner with the family today. Since his mother hadn't been in church, she would probably be at the hospital with Wallace anyway, and Jeremy wasn't going there. He couldn't bring himself to take up where he'd left off. It didn't seem natural. None of this seemed right or natural.

Closing his eyes, Jeremy sent up a prayer. *I need Your strength, Lord. I need to feel Your love. Help me make things right again. Help me find my purpose here.*

He opened his eyes to find Gabi Valencia and her girls exiting the church. He'd been both surprised and cautious about seeing her again, since he'd never divulged his identity to her. She looked pretty in her sensible brown coat and long corduroy skirt, her hands holding on to her daughters on either side. The maternal scene stood out in sharp contrast to Jeremy's rebellious thoughts. On impulse, he hurried to greet her.

"Hello," he said, waiting at the bottom of the steps.

"Hi."

Her greeting was short and distant. And he thought he knew the reason why.

"I never did introduce myself," he said, hoping she'd give him a chance to explain. "I'm Jeremy Hamilton."

The two little girls gazed down at him with wide-eyed curiosity, while their mother looked everywhere but at him.

She finally lifted her head, disappointment and distrust in her eyes. "No introductions needed now, Mr. Hamilton."

"Jeremy," he said. "I'm Jeremy. And as I said the other day, it's complicated."

"And none of my business," she replied, already distracted as one of her pretty little daughters ran off with some playmates. "Talia, we have to go."

The child kept on running. "Veronica, go get your sister and take her to the car," Gabriela said, pushing the other girl toward the cluster of kids prancing around the parking lot.

"I'm Roni," the one she'd called Veronica said to Jeremy. "I'm the oldest."

Gabi shook her head, a wry mother's smile turning up her mouth. "Which you remind everyone of constantly," she said. "Now, scoot."

"Nice to meet you, Roni," Jeremy said, taking the girl's hand to shake it.

The slender girl giggled, pulling away to hurry after her sister.

"They're both lovely," Jeremy said, not willing to give up just yet. "Like their mother."

She looked back at him then. But the smile was gone. Her expression held doubt, her dark eyes going cynical. "Thank you."

Feeling awkward and completely at a loss for words, Jeremy looked around. "I'd like to meet your husband."

She lifted her head, her eyes filling with a deep pain. "I…I'm a widow. My husband…died a few years ago."

"Oh, I'm sorry," Jeremy said, understanding that sadness in her eyes. "I don't know what to say."

"You don't have to say anything," she replied, a soft smile lifting her full lips. "It was good to see you again."

She moved to go after her girls, but Jeremy reached out a hand to stop her. "I'm sorry I didn't tell you who I was. I just needed…some time."

She seemed to absorb that as her distant stance changed and a flicker of compassion came into her eyes. "I understand. Being a Hamilton probably does carry a lot of complications."

He nodded, feeling the gentle censure in that remark. "You know all about me, I'm sure. So I can honestly say that in my case, *not* being a Hamilton carries even more complications. But I hope you won't hold that against me."

Her eyes widened at his implied remark. "Oh, no. You think—you must think—Mr. Hamilton, I mean, Jeremy, it never occurred to me—"

"It's okay. Everyone's curious. It's understandable you'd be put off by all the scandal surrounding me. I guess my coming to church today wasn't such a great idea, after all."

He turned to leave, his heart hurting with the weight of his shame. And the weight of her rejection.

"Jeremy?"

He heard her call out. He stopped, but refused to turn around.

"I don't back off very easily," she said in a soft voice as she came closer. "And I don't judge too harshly. You could have told me who you were the other day. It wouldn't have mattered to me."

He looked back then, caught up in her understanding gaze. "I appreciate that, at least. And I hope to see you again."

She didn't respond in words, but she did smile. It was a bittersweet smile, as if to say, "Sure, we'll see each other again, but that's about it."

It was obvious they were from two very different worlds. It was also obvious that Jeremy had too much baggage surrounding him to let a nice woman like Gabriela Valencia get involved in his problems. She'd told him everything he needed to know. She was a working mother and a widow. She was a faithful churchgoer who didn't want a man like him in her life. She was nice, pretty, polite, and way out of the realm of possibilities, because Jeremy wasn't ready for anything near serious with a woman, and because this particular woman's whole attitude toward him had changed now that she knew he was a Hamilton, or rather, now that she had found out he was *the* Hamilton.

The one everyone was talking about, the one everyone was feeling sorry for. He could certainly understand her hesitancy and her doubt. He had too much to get straight in his personal life before he plunged into any kind of relationship.

That much was apparent.

But something else was also apparent to Jeremy. Gabi Valencia represented the beautifully chaotic, homey existence he'd somehow lost out on, the kind of life he'd only dreamed about. But he'd always put that kind of life on hold, all for the sake of Hamilton Media. Those days were over, maybe for good.

For the first time in months, Jeremy had something, someone, other than himself and his family to focus on. He liked Gabi. He was intrigued by her, he was interested in her. And he really did hope to see her again. Very soon.

Chapter Three

Bright and early Monday morning, Jeremy stood in front of the Hamilton Media building, memories floating through his mind with the same drifting rhythm as the puffy clouds moving through the sky over Main Street.

Standing here now, he recalled in vivid detail the first time his father had brought him to this building. Jeremy must have been around five or so, and for months, he'd been begging Wallace to take him to the newspaper office. Wallace had always had an excuse.

"You'll get in the way, son."

"I'm too busy today, son. Maybe another time."

Finally, one morning at the breakfast table, her teacup in hand, his mother had gently pleaded with Wallace to take Jeremy to work.

"Show our son what you do all day, darling. Show him the legacy of Hamilton Media. After all, it'll all be his someday."

"His—and his brother's and sister's, too," Wallace had replied, his eyes still on his paper.

There had only been three Hamilton children then—Jeremy, Tim and tiny baby Amy. The twins and Melissa hadn't even been born. But they'd all learned at very early ages about the Hamilton legacy, about how Jeremy's namesake Jeremiah had started the *Davis Landing Dispatch* in the 1920s and had carried it through both the Depression and the Second World War. It was just *assumed* that every Hamilton child would be a part of this legacy.

At such a young age, however, Jeremy hadn't been sure just what a legacy was, but he'd been very sure that his father didn't want to take him to the office that day. He could still remember the whispered words between his parents, his father seeming stubborn and defiant, his mother, as always, gentle and persuasive. Finally, Wallace had given in, perhaps because his father had one soft spot and that was his wife.

Jeremy closed his eyes now, remembering the smells that had hit him when he'd entered the revolving doors to the lobby with his father. The aged, musty scents of antiques and old leather had mingled with the more modern smells of copier ink, new carpet and steel and plastic cubicles.

Then he'd heard the sounds: The ringing of many different telephones, the click-click of typewriters, and the easy, chaotic banter of reporters and editors had all assaulted Jeremy at once. It was an adrenaline rush that he'd never forgotten.

From the time he'd entered the building, the stain of printer's ink had settled over Jeremy like a mantle. He'd figured out what the word *legacy* must mean. It meant power. He'd seen that as his father hurried to the old, rickety elevator and headed to his plush office on the third floor. He'd felt that when Wallace barked orders and had people scurrying to do his bidding, from his prim secretary bringing him fresh coffee and the *Wall Street Journal*, to the nervous staffers who knocked on his door bringing him many questions. Everything here flowed through Wallace Hamilton. Jeremy had been in awe of that.

And he'd also clung to his father's every word, since Wallace rarely had time to spend with his oldest son. But on this day, only for today, Wallace had given Jeremy his undivided attention, simply by letting Jeremy watch him work. Wallace hadn't explained or lectured or hinted at what was required of Jeremy. But Jeremy had immediately understood. And, still in awe, he'd sat quietly, trying very hard not to bother his busy, powerful father. Jeremy watched and listened and learned, all the while being taken care of by his father's willing staff. If Jeremy wanted something, it immediately materialized. If he whimpered or whined, he was instantly hushed and handled.

But that day, as Jeremy had sat at his father's feet playing with an old ink stamp, he'd been hooked. As he'd grown older and found any excuse to come to work with Wallace more and more, he became caught up in wanting to spend all of his time here in this powerful, exciting place. Jeremy became a part of Hamilton Media by showing up whenever he could to help out, to learn, to absorb every nuance of this place and the work that happened here. His father had noticed, had grudgingly approved, and... Jeremy had simply slipped into place as second in command.

He loved the way the *Dispatch* brought news to people, and the way *Nashville Living* magazine informed and enlightened people. He loved the way the reporters worked day and night, getting their facts, gathering their information. He loved the way a deadline hit, all chaotic and full of stress, to be followed by a long, collective sigh of relief that filtered all the way down from his father's office to the lobby at day's end.

Now he missed the fast-paced confusion of a work day, and the satisfied feeling of getting the job done.

Now, he didn't know his place in the overall scheme of day-to-day life here at Hamilton Media. So he just stood, remembering, afraid to step back, afraid to move forward.

He stood and imagined Tim up there in the third-floor office that had once been Jeremy's. Tim, so driven, so intense, was in love. *Tim in love.* Jeremy shook his head at that particular paradox. So many things had happened in a few short months. He thought about Amy and how focused she could be on any task, and how hard she must be working now that she was in charge of *Nashville Living*, even with her high-school sweetheart Bryan back in her life. He smiled at thoughts of sweet, shy Heather finding the man of her dreams, and her twin, police officer Chris, falling in love with an independent female reporter for the *Dispatch*. He worried about Melissa, hoped she was settled now that she had Richard as her husband-to-be. He'd missed out on so much with all his siblings. He'd come back for that reason. He loved his family, in spite of everything. He needed his family, in spite of everything.

He lifted his head, the memories receding as the bright morning sun hurt his eyes. He knew he'd been standing here a full five minutes. He needed to go inside, visit with the Gordons. They'd be there to greet him, as they greeted everyone who entered this building. They'd be surprised, but polite and professional, as they'd been since the day Jeremy had met both of them.

Back then, Herman had been in charge of circulation and Louise had overseen the classifieds. What a formidable team. Much later, Jeremy and his brothers and sisters had dubbed them "the Gargoyles" because no matter their positions—and they'd both had many—the Gordons were loyal to Hamilton Media. They watched over this building and its occupants with iron-clad awareness. Long ago, they'd spoiled Jeremy with lollipops and chocolate. He imagined even now Louise would give him a wink and a lollipop, her way of solving all the world's problems.

Jeremy only wished it were that simple.

Taking a deep breath, he tried to calm himself. A silent prayer worked its way through the turmoil inside his brain. Once, prayer had come naturally to Jeremy; now it felt foreign and stilted. And yet, it was there.

I need help here, Lord. I need to find my way back, not just into this building, but back into the family I love. I need to forgive, Lord. I don't know how to ask, but I hope You hear me. I need my life back.

Maybe that life needs to be different now, came the gentle voice.

Jeremy glanced around, sure he looked ridiculous standing there, his mouth open in a gasp.

"You'll get more work done if you go inside the building."

He looked up to see Dawn Leroux coming toward him, her arms full of files and papers.

"You think so?" he said, managing a weak smile for the pretty blonde. Dawn had been a guiding light in the midst of all his angst and confusion. His brother was blessed to have her in his life.

She looked very feminine in her crisp white blouse and baby-blue flared skirt. Very different from his brother's usual girlfriends. But then, Jeremy reminded himself, his brother had changed.

Dawn stopped as she reached the door, her expression full of challenge. "What are you waiting for?"

"I'm not sure," he replied, glad for an understanding, objective friend. "But while I'm trying to figure that out, I ought to tell you that I've been on the job at the church already. The daycare room has one coat of paint—sloppy and spotty—but paint, none-theless."

"So I heard," she said, her smile as gentle as her eyes. "My friend Gabi gives you very high marks."

"How do you know Gabi?"

He hated the excitement in his voice. He didn't want to be excited. He didn't want anyone to see him excited.

"We've been friends for years," Dawn replied, shifting her load, her tone matter-of-fact and low-key. "We've gotten even closer since we both vol-unteer for a lot of the same programs at church."

He'd never noticed either of them at church, Jeremy thought now. He'd been too caught up in his work, in his life, in his *position,* to put much thought into who sat behind him in church. Now, he was very curious. So much had changed. He needed to keep pace with all of it.

And he needed to know more about Gabi.

"Give me that," he said, reaching to take Dawn's files. In spite of his curiosity, he changed the sub-ject to save grace. "I see my brother has you doing after-hours work."

"I don't mind," she replied, her eyes lighting up. "It's part of my job, and besides, I kinda know how the boss operates." Then she grinned. "Tell me more about you and Gabi."

"Nothing to tell," Jeremy said, warning bells going off in his head. *Could this woman read minds?* "She seems like a nice lady." *Explain her to me,* he silently begged.

Dawn complied. "The best. She's been through a rough time lately."

"She told me she's a widow. That must be horrible. I mean, she's still so young."

Dawn's eyes lost some of their light. "It's been hard on her and the girls, but Gabi has a strong faith. Of course, the holidays are always the worst, but she'll get through Christmas. She always tries to make it special for the girls."

Jeremy took in that information, then nodded. He wouldn't press Dawn to give him any more details. That didn't seem right. "I can see that—I mean, she seems like a great mom." Then he glanced toward the doors of the building, dread blocking out everything else. "Which is why she doesn't need someone like me in her life."

Now why in the world had he even said that? Too late, he saw the spark of interest in Dawn's eyes. And the spark of hope.

"You might be wrong there," Dawn retorted, pushing at the door. "You might be exactly what she needs in her life right now."

With that, she left Jeremy standing there holding the files. But she turned once inside. "You coming in?"

He nodded at her through the revolving doors, still stunned by her remarks. "I guess I am."

* * *

"So, have you made up your mind?"

Jeremy stood looking out the window of his brother Tim's office, watching the river just beyond the bluffs. Glancing over his shoulder, he saw Tim swiveling his chair to face him, his eyebrows raised.

"No, not yet," he said, turning back to the view.

Jeremy had toured the whole building, visiting with employees and family members alike, talking to each of them about how things were going. The place had kept on running without him, and he still wasn't so sure that's the way it should stay—without him. At least, he'd spent the better part of this morning trying to figure out if he even wanted to come back here.

But here he was, in the office at the top of the building. The office he used to occupy. And his brother was probably wondering the same thing. Did Jeremy really belong here? That was the question of the day.

For the last half hour, they'd tried to have a conversation. But as usual, Tim had been interrupted at least three times with one crisis after another. Tim thrived on crises and seemed to be handling all the balls he had to juggle with precision and decisiveness. Including what to do about his older brother's return.

"Jeremy, are you listening to me?"

Jeremy cringed, thinking he'd once been that man. The one who came just after Wallace Hamilton himself—second in command. The one who asked the questions and got immediate answers. Now, he only commanded curious stares from the lobby to the newsroom and beyond.

Right now, his brother was staring at him, eager and impatient for an answer. "This shouldn't be that hard."

"No, it shouldn't be," Jeremy agreed, "but I'm not sure what I'm doing here." He took a seat across from his brother, reluctant to be back in this office without being in the big chair, even if he had doubts about taking over again. "I keep thinking about the first time I came to this building with Da—with Wallace. I can't seem to get past that."

"I told you, you can have any position you want," Tim responded, his tone firm but aggravated. But his eyes held a kind of understanding that was new and fresh. "I'm trying here, Jeremy."

"I understand that." Jeremy glanced at the neat, organized desk, itching to get his hands on today's layout, longing to read over the editorials, to check the feature stories. Tim had everything lined up, ready to go. "I just don't know what position I need to be in right now, Tim." He drummed his fingers on the leather-covered arm of his chair. "You seem born to this. I'd hate to just up and take that away."

The silent message hummed between them. Tim *had* been born to this. Jeremy had stumbled into it because of a deep, dark secret and his birth order. How could he take up where he'd left off?

"I do like it," Tim finally admitted. At Jeremy's

questioning look, he added, "Okay, that was probably an understatement. I love it. But there are days—"

"I remember those days," Jeremy replied, relaxing back into the chair. "I never realized that I probably needed some time off. I just never dreamed I'd be forced out in such a jolting way."

"Nobody forced you," Tim reminded him. "You quit."

Jeremy kept drumming his fingers. No need to relive the vivid details. "So I did."

Tim leaned back, then pressed his hands behind his head, his fingers entwined. "There is something you could do, Jeremy, for all of us. I could use some help trying to figure out who's behind all these scandals."

Jeremy nodded, glad to have something, anything, to focus on. "I've gone back and studied all the leaks. It's obvious someone is deliberately giving juicy tidbits about our family to the *Observer*. That part is a no-brainer. Whoever it is, they're very much aware that the *Observer* is our rival. But what do they hope to gain by all of this?"

"They want to see us fall, or bring us down a peg or two," Tim replied, bringing his hands back to his desk with a slap. "This all started with you—or, at least, you finding out about your birth father."

Jeremy tried not to take that comment personally, but it was very personal. "So you think it might be someone close to me, or someone who knows all the inside information that only our family should know?"

Tim shrugged. "That makes sense, doesn't it?"

It did, but Jeremy rankled at that suggestion. "Yes, but that could apply to any one of us, Tim. It could be someone wanting to get back at Chris, maybe someone he arrested or testified against. Maybe someone wanting to sabotage *Nashville Living* just to bring down our subscriber base. Maybe it's someone at the *Observer,* trying to win points with the boss."

"All possibilities," Tim said, his tone guarded. "It might even be someone who works for us, hoping to get a better offer over at the *Observer.* We all know competition is fierce in this business." Then he shook his head. "Whoever this is—they want to embarrass our family by leaking personal details. And so far, they've succeeded. I still think it has something to do with our parents hiding the truth about your paternity. It's gone downhill from there."

Was his brother still trying to pin the blame for all their woes on Jeremy? He pushed that thought aside. "I don't think all of this is just coincidence, so you might be right. But as far as I know, none of us has any enemies in this town." Then he let out a sigh. "Unless someone is upset that I know who my birth father is now. Who would have anything to lose or gain from that though? He's dead and my grandparents live far away. It can't be that."

Tim looked as frustrated as Jeremy felt. "Whoever it is has his ear to the ground, that's for sure. They seem to find out personal things about us before we even know ourselves. I'd sure like to put an end to this, especially since Dad will be coming home soon. He doesn't need this kind of stress right now."

Jeremy didn't respond to that. He was still furious with his father. He wanted Wallace to beat the leukemia, but Jeremy wasn't ready to get all touchy-feely with Wallace.

"Are you ever going to forgive him?" Tim asked, just as the phone rang. He grabbed the receiver, then said into the phone, "Hold on a minute." Looking back at Jeremy, he waited with a hand over the phone.

"I'm working on it," Jeremy said. "And I'm leaving now. You're way too busy to keep me company."

"I don't mind," Tim said, but he was already waving Jeremy out the door as he gave brisk answers to the person on the other end of the line. "Okay, kill the city council update until we have a confirmation, and go with the proposal for the new factory near the river. And I want details—environmental and economical impact, the works."

Jeremy emerged from the privacy of his brother's office to find himself in limbo, standing in the middle of the long hallway just outside Dawn's office area. Dawn wasn't at her desk, so chatting with her wasn't an option.

When did I become so needy for company? he wondered.

Then he heard the elevator swishing open, his mind going toward escape. Hurrying to catch the door, he ran right smack into the person coming out.

Instinctively, Jeremy reached his hands up to keep from colliding with the petite woman.

And looked down to find Gabi Valencia in his arms.

"Oh, oh, I'm so sorry," Gabi said, gazing up into Jeremy Hamilton's intense blue eyes. She couldn't move. He held her there, frozen in her tracks. "It's you again."

"Me again," he said, stepping back, his hands dropping to his side, his expression full of surprise and maybe, approval. "I seem to see you everywhere I go these days."

"It's a small town," she said, glancing beyond him as she willed her heartbeat to a calm, workable level. "I'm meeting Dawn for lunch. Have you seen her?"

He looked bemused, then disappointed. "You're sure in a hurry to get away from me, aren't you?"

Gabi felt the heat of a blush coloring her skin. "No. I'm just…running a little late." She waved her hands in the air. "It was crazy at the hospital today."

"You work at Community General?"

"Yes. In administration. Behind the scenes."

"That must keep you busy."

"Yes. And it pays the bills."

She looked past him again. If Dawn didn't show up soon, she'd have to get something to eat without her in order to make it back to work on time. She really didn't need to be standing here making small talk with Jeremy Hamilton, either.

Trying to be polite, she said, "I'm sorry, I've got to find Dawn and scoot."

"Okay." His skeptical look told her she hadn't fooled him one bit. "I was just leaving anyway. And I'm not sure where Dawn is right now."

"Here I am," came the breathless reply.

Gabi breathed a sigh of relief as she saw Dawn rushing toward them. "Hi."

"Hi," Dawn said through a long sigh. "Sorry. Last-minute orders from the Typhoon."

They both giggled, then Gabi shot a look toward Jeremy.

Dawn shrugged. "Jeremy knows how Tim can be, right, Jeremy?"

Gabi saw a slight smile fighting to break through on Jeremy's handsome face. "Is my hyper brother causing woe around here?"

"Always," Dawn replied, taking Gabi by the arm. "Let's get out of here before he barks something else at me."

When she grabbed Jeremy with her other arm, both he and Gabi stopped to stare at each other.

"What?" Dawn asked, all coy and innocent. "Jeremy, don't you need to eat? We're going over to Betty's Bake Shoppe. Might as well come with us, since *my* date is too busy to eat." She lifted her head toward Tim's office. "I'll have to bring him takeout again." Then she turned to Gabi. "You don't mind, do you, Gabi?"

What could Gabi say to her friend? Yes, she did mind? Yes, she'd love to have lunch with Jeremy

Hamilton? No, she couldn't possibly have lunch with this man? Well, she couldn't be rude, could she?

Both Jeremy and Dawn were waiting for her answer. One with a knowing smile, and the other one—well, his perfectly blank expression gave nothing away. But his eyes held a hint of hope. And challenge.

Remembering Dawn's suggestion that Jeremy could use a friend, Gabi shot him a wan smile, while she poked Dawn in the ribs. "Of course not. It's just lunch. And we're wasting precious minutes, standing here."

Dawn pushed the elevator button. "Good. I'm starving."

Gabi got in behind Dawn, hoping she'd be able to eat. It might be hard, with a Hamilton man sitting across the table. Jeremy stood there, staring at them.

"Jeremy, are you coming with us?" Dawn asked, grinning.

Jeremy looked directly at Gabi. "I don't want to intrude."

Dawn, for once, stayed quiet. But she quirked a brow toward Gabi.

"You're not intruding," Gabi finally said, sure she'd regret this later. "Please, join us."

He stepped into the elevator and silently pushed the button to the lobby, his gaze moving over Dawn's smiling face before his eyes settled on Gabi. Then he gave her that hesitant little half smile she was beginning to recognize. "Lunch with two lovely women. I think my day just got a whole lot better."

Chapter Four

Jeremy's good mood changed the minute they entered Betty's Bake Shoppe and Bookstore. The crowded dining area went still as everyone in town, it seemed, glanced up and right at him. The silence that followed only added to his humiliation. He wanted to turn around and leave, but one glance at Gabi and he knew he couldn't do that.

She sent him a challenging look, followed by a soft smile. "You're a Hamilton, remember? Act like one."

Surprised at the spunk behind that whispered statement, he actually managed to smile back. "But they all know the truth," he said through gritted teeth. "Maybe I should just—"

"Don't you dare," Dawn said, giving him her own determined look.

Gabi stood on one side and Dawn on the other, closing ranks around him. Dawn leaned close. "The truth is that you will always be Jeremy Hamilton. Are you gonna let the gossips win?"

Jeremy mulled that over, his head coming up, his gaze scanning the crowd. He might be confused and disillusioned, but he'd never been a coward. Nodding, he lifted his head even higher and met the compassionate gaze of Betty Owens herself.

"Jeremy Hamilton," Betty said, a nervous lilt to her greeting. "C'mon on in here and let me get you something to eat."

Jeremy breathed a sigh of relief. Betty had never been chummy with him, but she'd always been polite at least. "Thanks, Betty. It's good to see you."

"Good to have you back." Betty fidgeted with the menus, her head down. "Y'all can have a table near the window. I'll send Justine over to take your order in just a jiffy."

Jeremy had always admired Betty's work ethic. She was a fixture here at the Bake Shoppe, greeting customers, smiling and comparing good stories with the many book buyers. She also loved to tell juicy stories too, mostly gossip. Betty always knew anything around town before anyone else did. Maybe he should have a long talk with her. She might know who'd been leaking all these scandals to the *Observer*.

Then a thought occurred to him. Could it be Betty? No, that wasn't possible. She might like to gossip, but Betty Owens would never deliberately hurt another human being with malicious intent. In fact, she'd always been a bit close-mouthed and standoffish regarding the Hamiltons.

Which made Jeremy even more curious, now that

he thought about it. He appreciated her business sense as well as her book smarts. But he'd never figured out why she always seemed so distant and nervous around him, as if she couldn't open up with him the way she did with most of her customers. Today, she looked tired. *Drained* was a better word. Maybe she just needed a break. He could certainly understand that concept.

Glancing around after Betty walked away, Jeremy ignored the stares and whispers, concentrating instead on the few friends who took the time to wave and smile at him.

His brother Chris's partner on the police force, Jason Welsh, called out from the next table. "Jeremy, you old hound dog. Chris said you were home. Good to see you."

"Thanks, Jason," Jeremy said, waving a hand. "Where's my brother today, anyway?"

Jason's smile lit up his face. "He's with Felicity. Those two are an item, don't you know?"

"I do know," Jeremy replied, happy for his baby brother. His half brother, he reminded himself.

He turned back to find Gabi staring at him, a pleased expression on her pretty face.

"See, it's not so bad," she said, her dark eyes watching him with an intensity that almost made him feel even more uncomfortable. Except that he saw no hint of pity in her eyes. More like admiration and pride.

She shrugged it off. "We've all been the center of gossip at one time or another."

"It's not easy," he admitted, wondering when in her life she'd been in this kind of situation.

"No one is going to mess with you," Dawn said, her tone indicating she wouldn't allow that.

Jeremy sighed, then pretended to read over the menu.

"You two make a formidable team, but I can handle this." He dropped the menu, his gaze moving over Gabi. "Thank you."

Gabi sent him a warm, shy smile. "I owe you, remember?"

"You do?"

"Yes. You single-handedly painted the church daycare and nursery, didn't you?"

He chuckled. "Yeah, and most of the floor and myself, too."

"You did a great job, Jeremy," Dawn said, nodding her approval. "But don't get too comfortable. Your work at church is not done yet."

He groaned. "Is that why you insisted on bringing me to lunch? So you could bribe me into more hard labor?"

"Maybe," Dawn said, grinning. "Hmmm. I think I'll have a chicken salad sandwich. How about you, Gabi?"

Jeremy waited, watching Gabi's face as she studied the menu. "My usual, probably. A vegetable plate."

"She thinks she has to watch her weight," Dawn pointed out to Jeremy.

Jeremy gave Gabi another once-over. Her long

dark hair fell around her shoulders in gentle waves. Her blue button-up sweater was a nice contrast to her crisp white blouse. Her clothes were nothing fancy, not like the designer outfits his sisters and his mother wore in various forms and fashions, but she looked dainty and feminine just the same.

"You look fine to me," he said, then quickly averted his eyes to glance out the window. He hadn't meant that to slip out.

Gabi looked down at her menu, clearly embarrassed. "My mother is an excellent cook, and I rarely have time to exercise. I have to be careful."

Dawn shook her head. "You get plenty of exercise, running after those two girls." Then she waved a hand in the air toward Jeremy. "Oh, you should try Mrs. Marquez's tamales, Jeremy. They are *so* good." Lifting her brow, she turned to Gabi. "Think your mom would feed this poor man?"

Jeremy gave Gabi a mock-pathetic look, just to see if he could make her blush again. "I do love tamales."

"You'd have to get in line," Gabi said, very pragmatically. "I have four brothers and a sister. We know the boardinghouse reach very well at my parents' table."

"I know that same reach, even if I was only allowed to do that whenever my mother wasn't looking," Jeremy said, then he looked down at the table. "Although it's been a while since I've been to a Hamilton family dinner."

"All the more reason to try dinner somewhere

else for a change," Dawn suggested, shrugging. "You don't have to mind your manners so much at the Marquez house."

"We have manners," Gabi said, grinning. Then she looked from him to Dawn, clearly confused at her friend's suggestion. "My mother will feed anyone who wants a good meal, though."

Jeremy laughed again. "Such a nice way of saying c'mon by anytime, right? I think I get the picture. Maybe I'd better stick to my own family dinners, even though they can be a bit stuffy at times."

Gabi was about to answer when Betty's daughter, Justine, came over to take their orders. "Hi," she said, her tone low. "What can I get y'all today?"

Jeremy let the women order first, then said, "I'll have the Betty Burger, with the works."

Justine smiled down at him, her eyes holding his for a minute, some unreadable emotion there in their depths. "Glad you're home, Jeremy."

Jeremy thanked her, then turned to Gabi and Dawn after Justine walked away. "Is it just me, or are the Owens women acting a bit odd today?"

Gabi shrugged. "You know how Betty likes to gossip. Maybe she's just trying to keep her thoughts to herself for once. So you won't feel awkward."

"Regarding my paternity?" he asked, comfortable enough to be honest with these two at least.

"That and all the other rumors about the Hamiltons," Dawn replied. "I guess you've heard the latest one, right?"

Jeremy glanced around then lowered his voice.

"You mean, about my father possibly having an illegitimate child out there somewhere? Yes, I've heard and if I get my hands on the person spreading this stuff—"

He looked up to find Justine standing there with a tray full of tea glasses, her eyes centered on him. The look she gave him this time was full of doubt and anxiety.

Jeremy had to wonder if maybe Betty and Justine knew something he didn't know, after all. But then, that was nothing new around here, he thought with a bitter resolve. He'd promised Tim he'd try to look into this mess. Maybe he should start right here at Betty's Bake Shoppe.

He waited for Justine to put down their drinks, then glanced over at Gabi. "Maybe coming here was a bad idea."

"No, it wasn't," she said. She leaned close enough for him to get a faint whiff of her exotic perfume. "You have nothing to be ashamed about, Jeremy. Nothing at all."

Her words held a conviction Jeremy couldn't feel. "I'm not used to being the center of gossip," he said. "This has all been very difficult—for my entire family." He thought of his mother and how she'd held her head high throughout his father's illness, through all the rumors and embarrassing gossip. Then he thought of Wallace, a shard of piercing guilt hitting his heart. He pushed that guilt away, not ready to examine it just yet. "People don't stop to think how this is hurting my mother. She's done nothing to deserve this kind of pain."

"I know how that feels," Gabi replied. Then she looked away, her hands fluttering in the air. "I mean, nobody likes to be talked about. Especially when half the people talking don't know the truth."

Jeremy didn't ask her how she knew this. First-hand experience, maybe? Her words only added to her mystique and allure. He wondered again about that trace of sadness he'd seen now and then in her dark eyes. She was probably still mourning her husband.

He looked over at Dawn, and saw an encouraging expression on her face. Then Dawn said, "Let's change the subject. Let's talk about Melissa and Richard's wedding. Gabi, are you coming?"

"I hadn't thought about it," Gabi said. "I thought it was only for family, considering the circumstances."

"Yet another family scandal to overcome," Jeremy retorted.

"Oh, I didn't mean it that way," Gabi quickly replied. "I—I just wouldn't want to interfere. I'm sorry, Jeremy, but I don't know your family very well."

Jeremy wanted to tell her he'd like to remedy that, but he didn't. Instead he said, "You just know *of* us. I hope you won't hold that against us. We're actually quite normal."

Gabi shook her head. "No family is completely normal. Mine is no exception. My poor parents have spent many sleepless nights worrying about all of us." Her eyes went dark again, as if she was remembering bad times.

Jeremy wanted to know more, but he didn't push the issue. "Well, this wedding is certainly not traditional. My sister is pregnant and marrying a man eleven years older than her. Our family lawyer, no less! Talk about gossip and scandal." Then he shrugged. "As for me, I'm so glad Melissa has found a good man who can love her in spite of her past mistakes."

As he said that, he couldn't help but think of his own mother and Wallace. Wallace was a good man and he loved Nora. Jeremy couldn't ask for more than that. Except…he wanted more. He had to work on that want, he decided. His parents had done what they believed to be right at the time, and he'd had a good life because of their love for each other. Maybe it was time for him to get over his hurt and get on with being part of the family again.

"She's invited, right, Jeremy?" Dawn asked, her expression telling him to back her up.

Gabi held up a hand. "To the wedding? No, really, I don't expect—"

"Of course," Jeremy said. "We'd love to have you there."

He didn't add that he'd be happy to escort Gabi himself. He wasn't that bold yet. And he wasn't so sure he'd even be at the wedding. But he had a feeling if sassy Dawn Leroux had her way, however, both Gabi and he would be attending.

Together.

* * *

Behind the counter, Betty exchanged a worried look with Justine. "Do you think he might suspect?"

"I don't know," Justine said, her voice low and quiet. "And besides, I told you it doesn't matter to me."

"But it might matter to the other Hamilton children," Betty said. "Especially if they find out the whole truth."

"They won't," Justine assured her. "Everything is going to be all right, Mama. I'm sure of it."

Betty smiled at her daughter, doubt coloring her expression. "We have to trust in God, honey. That's all we can do now."

The man sitting near them at the counter only smiled and continued to read his paper. He'd learned how to blend in so well, people forgot he was even around. A man could learn a lot of information that way, simply by staying still and quiet. He couldn't help but overhear some of Betty and Justine's conversation—just enough to make him put two and two together. And he couldn't help the gloating feeling that came over him as he watched Jeremy Hamilton leave the restaurant. This sure made up for the fact that Hamilton hadn't even recognized or acknowledged him when he'd come strutting into Betty's with those two good-looking women. But then, the mighty Hamiltons would have a lot to make up for before this was over. He'd see to that.

"Could you be any more obvious?" Gabi whispered to Dawn after they parted ways with Jeremy on the street corner. After thanking them for lunch, he'd told them he planned on spending some time with his mother this afternoon.

"I don't know what you're talking about," Dawn said, her expression all innocence.

"Oh, yes, you do," Gabi said, watching as Jeremy drove away in a sleek gray Mercedes. He flashed them a big smile, then waved. "You practically asked the man to take me to that wedding."

"I merely suggested you were invited," Dawn replied. "You don't have to go."

"I'm sure I won't," Gabi said, relaxing a little now that Jeremy was gone. But she had to admit she'd enjoyed their lunch together, even if she did get funny feelings inside her stomach every time she was around him. "I mean, I've got shopping to do before Christmas. We've got the play at church and both my girls have parts in that. I've got cookies to bake, gifts to find and wrap. I don't see how I can find the time—"

"You like him, don't you?" Dawn asked, grinning.

"Of course I like the man. He's polite and well-mannered and, well, he's just lonely. Yes, I like him. But I don't know him well enough to…consider going to his sister's wedding with him." She shifted on her boot heels. "Besides, since when did a working-class girl from across the tracks even consider hanging with a Hamilton man, Dawn?"

"I'm doing it," Dawn replied smartly.

Gabi nudged her with an elbow. "Well, that certainly doesn't mean I have to follow suit."

"But—"

"But, nothing. It's not even within the realm of possibility. Me and Jeremy Hamilton, yeah, right."

And yet, Gabi felt that warm sensation deep inside her stomach, that sensation that told her meeting Jeremy Hamilton was going to be significant to her life.

Why did the man make her so nervous and jittery? Maybe because he was good-looking and… just a tad tormented? No, she wouldn't let that happen to her again. She'd had to deal with one man's torment, leaving her feeling helpless. And when she'd realized the extent of Octavio's depression, it was too late. Much too late.

But Jeremy's not like your husband, she reminded herself. *He's just a friend. So far.*

As if sensing her distress, Dawn touched a hand to her arm. "I didn't mean to upset you. I just thought—"

"I know you had good intentions," Gabi said, patting Dawn's hand. "And I know since you are head-over-heels in love with Tim, naturally, you want the same for me. It's awfully sweet, but I'm a big girl. I can find my own way."

"I hope so," Dawn said. "I know so. But I'll try to stay out of your love life from now on."

"Thank you," Gabi said. "You have enough to keep you busy with Tim Hamilton."

"Speaking of," Dawn said, looking at her watch,

"I'd better get back to work before he sends out an all-points bulletin for his brother Chris to go look for me."

They both giggled at that. "Me, too," Gabi said, giving her friend a quick hug. "I'll see you later."

A tall, well-dressed man came out the door then, smiling at them with a wolfish set of blue eyes. "Ladies."

Dawn frowned, but didn't remark. Gabi didn't recognize the man, but she didn't like the way he'd looked at her either. "That was strange."

Dawn's cell phone rang. "Oh, got to go. The master calls." She laughed and shook her head. "If he wasn't so adorable—"

Gabi waved her away, then headed to her car, her mind on the many things she had to do before she went to bed that night. They were having dinner with her family at her sister Yolanda's house, so at least she wouldn't have to go home and cook. There was so much to keep her busy, so much to keep her occupied. She should be happy she had such a rich, full life in spite of being a widow and single mother.

She was content, and she loved her girls so much. She wanted to make Christmas special for them, just to keep herself from going into a depression of her own. She'd learned to accept that life and death were just part of God's plan. But it was times like this that she missed her husband so much. She missed having someone to hold her close, to hear her joys and her fears. She missed having a soul mate, a helpmate, a partner. And her well-meaning friends only made things worse by trying to "help" her find someone else.

She thought of Jeremy Hamilton, and wondered if he'd ever had any serious relationships. Wondered if he felt lonely and out of sorts at times, too. Surely he did now, coming home to face so much pain and scandal.

"And surely, it's none of your business, Gabriela," she said to herself. Then she gave herself a good talking-to in rapid Spanish, just as her mother used to whenever she thought Gabi was being ridiculous.

And she was being ridiculous, Gabi told herself. She had to put this…connection she felt to the rich and powerful Jeremy Hamilton out of her mind.

Somehow.

Chapter Five

"I'm so glad you came by."

Jeremy reached across the small mahogany table to touch his hand to his mother's frail-looking fingers. "I needed to find a quiet place, and when Vera Mae told me you were here…." He shrugged, leaving the statement hanging.

But his mother finished the thought for him. "You knew we could have a nice, private visit."

"Yes." Jeremy finished his coffee and pushed away the half-eaten pecan pie Vera Mae had insisted on bringing him.

They were in one of the front parlors. Jeremy had found his mother there, quietly playing an old hymn on the piano. She'd come home from the hospital to shower and rest for a few hours. That gave him enough time to visit with her before she headed back to Community General to sit with Wallace.

Nora patted his hand, her hazel eyes watering. "You should go see your father." Her expression begged him to see Wallace in that light. "He is still your father, Jeremy."

Jeremy looked out the window, his gaze moving over the well-tended lawn. All the fall leaves had been raked away. The holly shrubs were in fruit, their bright red berries indicating that soon it would be Christmas. This old house would be decorated and trimmed out in bright reds and vivid greens, the scent of evergreen and cinnamon wafting up the great hallway. His mother would put up a huge tree right here beside the grand piano and the whole family would gather to sing their favorite carols.

His heart hurt with the memories, both good and bad.

"Jeremy?"

Nora's voice called him back. She looked so tired. His mother was getting old, but she didn't look her age. He knew she had to be weary from sitting at the hospital day and night. Glad she'd come home for a while, he decided instead of answering her, he'd ask her a question of his own.

"Why don't you rest here tonight, Mother? We'll find someone to sit with him."

"Can't you even say it, Jeremy? Can't you call him Dad again, for my sake at least?"

Jeremy lowered his head, then ran a hand down the knotted muscles in the back of his neck. "I'm trying, Mom. I want to…get past this. But it's just not easy."

"Why don't you blame me, then?" Nora asked,

her hand still on his. "I was the one who got pregnant."

"It's not your fault."

"It *was* my fault. I loved Paul beyond reason. That kind of love can either be a blessing or it can be fatal."

He looked up and saw the raw pain in her eyes. He'd never stopped to consider how she must have suffered back then. So young, and at a time when the world was much more innocent and far less forgiving. "I think you've paid dearly for that past sin, Mother."

"I don't consider you a sin, son. But I have asked God to forgive me, and I dedicated my life to serving Him in return. If it hadn't been for your father—for Wallace, I don't know what you and I would have done."

Jeremy shut his eyes and let out a long sigh. "I understand that." Then he opened his eyes to stare at her. She was impeccably dressed, as usual. She wore a winter-white wool suit and the gleaming pearls she'd worn for as long as Jeremy could remember. She looked serene and petite, in spite of the dark circles underneath her eyes. "I've had a good life, Mom. The best. I've tried to make you proud—"

"And you have."

"But…it wasn't enough. You have to understand, it wasn't enough for him. He resented me. I can see that now. He wanted Tim—"

"He wanted you. He trained you to take his place

and you did a *fine job* at Hamilton Media. You should be there now."

Frustrated, but determined not to upset his mother, Jeremy got up to pace around the piano. "Tim is doing a fine job now. Maybe that's the way it should be."

"But what will you do?"

"That's the big question." He rocked back on his heels. "I was there this morning, but I'm still conflicted. I have to get readjusted. But I do believe that we should leave things in Tim's capable hands for now."

Nora got up, too, using the top of the gleaming piano for leverage. "But you will return one day, right?"

Jeremy pivoted to look down at his mother, then took her arm to help her away from the piano bench and around the occasional table he'd been sitting near. "I honestly don't know. Maybe after the holidays, after we're sure," he stopped, took a deep breath, "after we're sure Daddy is going to be all right."

Nora's eyes watered up again. "You called him Daddy. Oh, Jeremy, you have to forgive him. You have to forgive both of us."

Jeremy pulled his mother into his arms. "I'm working on that, Mom, I promise. But I think, mostly, I have to forgive myself. I shouldn't have quit that day. But it's done now."

Nora pulled back to look up at him, a pleading

expression on her face. "Will you go with me, back to the hospital?"

Jeremy backed away. He didn't want to hurt his mother, but he wasn't ready to face Wallace. "No. Not just yet. But soon."

Nora nodded, her eyes filling with tears again. "Well, I have to get back then. Chris and Felicity were there with your father when I left. They decided to have lunch with him at the hospital, but I know they can't stay all afternoon."

"Do you want me to drive you?"

"No. Since your father's been so sick, Tim arranged for a driver for me. That way I don't have to depend on any of you to bring me back and forth."

Jeremy gave her a soft smile. "Tim thinks of everything."

"He has changed, Jeremy. Dawn is a wonderful woman. She's helped him find his way back to God."

"She can be very forceful," Jeremy said, glad to be on a happier subject. "It won't be long before those two are walking down the aisle."

"We've had lots of happy times lately," Nora said, "in spite of your father's illness. There is always a blessing to be found in any situation. It's almost as if his being so sick has caused all of our children to want to settle down and make families of their own."

"Except your eldest here," Jeremy said, chuckling.

"Do you have anyone special in your life?" Nora

asked as he escorted her toward the back of the house.

Jeremy thought of Gabi Valencia, surprised that her face had flashed before him. But then, he'd just had lunch with her. "No, no one special right now. I've got too many issues to work through to think about women."

"I'll pray that you find someone soon, then," Nora told him. "And I'll keep praying for things to…change between your father and you."

"Thanks," Jeremy said, leaning down to kiss her. "And remember, take care of yourself."

"I'll be fine," Nora told him as she gathered her purse and coat. "Can I tell your father you stopped by?"

"I don't mind that one bit," Jeremy replied. "Tell him…just tell him that I'm here."

"I will," Nora said, waving bye.

Jeremy watched as the burly chauffeur who'd been sitting in the kitchen drinking coffee with Vera Mae escorted his mother out to the dark sedan parked in the back driveway.

Then he turned and headed to his own car, Vera Mae's call of "You take care, now," echoing in his mind right along with all the memories surrounding him.

She had so many good memories in this place.

Gabi heard the laughter as she entered the front door of her sister Yolanda's house. Her sister had married Pete Duffy two years ago, and they now lived in a mid-sized ranch-style house very similar to Gabi's own house, on the outskirts of Hickory Mills. It was beige brick and angular, nothing fancy, but to Gabi's middle-class, hard-working sister, it had seemed like a dream come true. A dream with a mortgage that Pete complained about on a weekly basis, but everyone knew he was happy here. Gabi expected her sister to announce any day that she was pregnant, since Yolanda and Pete wanted a family of their own.

"One day…" Gabi said as she hurried into the kitchen, the girls rushing ahead of her. And one day, maybe she'd also find a nice man herself, and settle down to finally pay off the mortgage on her own tiny house.

Stop that, Gabi told herself. You don't need a man in your life.

But she couldn't help but think of one particular man. The man she'd had lunch with just that day. He could probably pay off her mortgage with one check. All the more reason to put Jeremy Hamilton out of her mind for good. Even if he was going through a crisis, the man was still a wealthy Hamilton. Gabi didn't need his money, and she certainly didn't need him.

But, he sure was interesting to talk to and be with.

"Mama met a man," she heard Talia shout as she entered the noisy kitchen.

All the chatter ceased as every eye in the room turned to Gabi.

"What's this?" her mother Marisol asked, her thick Spanish accent ringing clear in the silence. "Who have you met, Gabriela?"

Gabi dropped the bowl of potato salad she'd made onto the counter, glared down at her youngest, then shrugged. "I meet men all the time, Mama."

"But you had lunch with this one," Veronica reminded her, her hands on her hips, her eyes full of mirth.

Gabi winced. Apparently her children had heard her talking to Dawn on the phone earlier. "Yes, so I did." She glanced around the room at the curious crowd of relatives. "I had lunch with Dawn and she invited someone else to go with us. So?"

"So, tell us everything," her sister said, grinning as she came around the counter lugging a pot of steaming chili. "Who is this mystery man?"

"He's rich," Talia said, dancing around in circles. "And he's so handsome. He smiled at me in church Sunday."

Yolanda mimicked Veronica, her hands on her hips. "Really now? Rich, handsome, and a church-goer. Sounds perfect to me." Then she leaned toward Gabi. "Tell us, Gabi."

Gabi lowered her head, gave her two grinning daughters a warning glare, then said, "It's Jeremy Hamilton."

Everyone started talking at once. She heard several superlatives in all the chatter, both in English and in Spanish. "Rich...for sure. *Sí*. Scandal...

rumors...powerful... Way out of our league... Little sister is running with the big dogs now, no doubt."

"Okay, enough," Gabi shouted, her gaze moving over her brothers. Juan Carlos looked worried, as any older brother would. Raul looked amused, as any ladies' man would, and Arturo seemed nonchalant as he grabbed a bag of chips and salsa and headed into the den to watch Monday-night football. Oscar stared at her as if she'd grown two heads.

"What?" she shouted, her own high spirits rising to the occasion. "Can't I have lunch with a man now and then?"

Her niece Sonia answered that. "Sure, Aunt Gabi. Especially when that man is a rich and handsome Hamilton. Wow, wait until I tell my friends at school—"

Gabi grabbed Sonia by the sleeve of her suede jacket. "There will be no telling of anything, understand? The man already has enough problems without my entire family gossiping about him. It was just lunch. Just one time. No big deal."

Her mother, petite and dark-skinned, touched an arm to Gabi's sweater. "Are you so sure about that? It might become a big deal."

Her father Juan nodded. "*Sì,* your mother is right. If you're seen with this man in public, you might become involved whether you want to or not."

"He's a friend," Gabi stated as she shooed her curious brothers and their various wives and girlfriends out of the room. "Just a friend, people. Now can we just eat and watch the game? I'm starved."

"Maybe because you were too nervous to eat lunch, huh?" Yolanda asked, grinning over at her smiling husband.

Pete held his hands up, then backed away. "I'm staying out of this one. If Gabi has a new man in her life, whether he's a Hamilton or not, I say more power to her. I'm so crazy in love, I want everybody to be happy."

Yolanda blew him a kiss. "Silly. Go in there and find a spot. I'll bring you a bowl of chili."

Somehow, between her mother and Yolanda, everyone was pushed out of the tiny kitchen and into the den where the talk went from Gabi to the game on television.

When the room grew quiet, Yolanda cornered Gabi by the refrigerator. "So, what's the real story on Jeremy Hamilton, sister?"

Gabi busied herself with filling glasses with ice. "There is no story. I just met him at church and now, well, we're getting to know each other. I rarely see the man."

"You never did before, that's for sure," Yolanda commented, helping to fill the glasses with tea and soda. "Why now?"

"I told you," Gabi said, feeling defensive. Her sister was her closest friend and confidante, but Gabi was afraid to voice her true feelings, even to Yolanda. "He volunteered to help paint the daycare at church and that's how we got to know each other. He just got back into town a few weeks ago."

"I've heard the rumors," Yolanda said, her keen

gaze on Gabi. "But I want to know what *you* think about him."

Gabi turned and leaned back against the counter. "He is handsome, no doubt about that," she admitted. "And of course, he has manners. But he's also a very nice person. He doesn't act rich, if you know what I mean."

"I think I do," Yolanda said, nodding. "I don't know the man, but from what I've heard around town, his brother Tim puts on more airs than Jeremy. Tim throws his weight around, but Jeremy is more cautious and quiet."

"That's true," Gabi said, reaching for the pan of cornbread their mother had baked. "But Tim's changed a lot over the last few months, too. He's had more responsibility since Jeremy left Hamilton Media and…he's in love with Dawn. If anyone could change a man for the better, it would be Dawn Leroux."

"I agree with you there," Yolanda said. "But I think my big sister could change a man, too. Maybe even a man like Jeremy Hamilton. I think you'd be good for him." Then she leaned close. "But…will he be good for you?"

"Thanks for the vote of confidence," Gabi said, "but honestly, we're just friends. Nothing more. So don't worry about me."

Gabi turned to find her mother's intense gaze centered on her. Marisol stepped closer, then took Gabi's hand in her own. "Be careful, daughter. We're different from the Hamiltons. I'd hate for you to get your hopes up. I don't want you to get hurt."

"I'll be okay, Mama," Gabi said, holding her mother's hand tight. "I'll be very careful. I have no illusions regarding Jeremy, trust me."

"I'll say a prayer for you," Marisol replied, "and for your new friend, too."

"We both could use that prayer," Gabi said. Then she hugged her mother close. "At least I know I have all of you. Jeremy is so alone right now."

"Then the rumor is true?" Marisol asked, her eyes going wide.

"I'm afraid it is, but it shouldn't matter. Jeremy will always be a Hamilton. He just needs to realize that."

"Would you still like him if he wasn't a Hamilton?" her mother asked.

Gabi thought about that for a minute, then nodded. "*Sì,* I think I would. I like what I see in Jeremy's heart."

"And what do you see there?"

"Goodness, kindness, a bit of humility, a little bit of arrogance. But…he is a good man. Nothing will change that. He just has to realize that for himself."

"Unless he grows bitter from all this talk."

"He is bitter. But we're working on changing that."

Marisol laughed. "You and who else?"

Gabi grinned, then kissed her mother on the cheek. "Me and God, of course."

"Amen to that, then," her mother said as they headed into the crowded den to eat with their family.

Gabi glanced around and thanked God for each and every one of her crazy but lovable relatives. And she did say a prayer for Jeremy. He needed his own family back in his life.

Maybe that was why God had put them together, so Gabi could show Jeremy his way back home again.

And in doing so, she might find some kind of inner strength to help her through her own lonely times, too.

What could be so wrong in that?

Chapter Six

A week later, Jeremy entered the Northside Community Church educational building and lifted his nose. Sniffing, he followed the wonderful smell into the long kitchen at the back of the fellowship hall.

"Cookies," he said, happy to find Gabi standing there with a spatula in one hand and a spoon in the other.

"Oh, good," she replied, waving the spoon at him. "You're just in time. Could you get the next batch out of the oven for me?"

"Sure," Jeremy said, smiling at her practical, no-nonsense bossiness. "But I want one of those cookies."

"You can have two if you'll help me finish cooking them," Gabi said as she lifted the fresh-baked sugar cookies off the baking tray then placed them along the waxed paper on the counter to cool. "And you get to help the girls and me decorate. They're due any minute from choir practice."

"More painting?" Jeremy said, careful to make

sure he had the potholders he'd found near the stove wrapped around the piping-hot baking pan in his hands. "You know that's not my specialty."

"I'll teach you," Gabi said, finally turning to smile at him. "Hi."

"Hi, yourself. Do you always show up here every day after work, or is my timing just that good?" He decided not to tell her why he was here. He'd let that be a nice surprise for later.

She dusted flour off her hands, then shrugged. "Actually, this particular task was supposed to be taken care of by two very dear ladies, but they're both sick with that nasty flu that's going around. I got a last-minute call from Dawn. She needs these cookies for her food deliveries—you know, to the people she services with her Meals-on-Wheels program?"

Jeremy nodded, noticing Gabi had flour on her face, too. It only added to her charm. "I've heard Tim mention that. Seems that's how he got to know Dawn. He helped her make some deliveries?"

"Yes, after he ran into her car."

"That would be Tim, always in a hurry."

"I think Dawn's taught him to slow down a bit."

"The Lord truly does work in mysterious ways."

"Indeed." She stood there, looking up at him, an expectant expression on her face. "How are things in that department for you?"

Jeremy grabbed a cookie. "You mean, between the Lord and me?"

"Yes, and between...your family and you?"

"You're certainly nosy."

She got all flushed. "I'm sorry. You're right. It's none of my business."

Jeremy reached out to wipe the flour off her cheek, causing her to lift her head. Her skin was warm, probably from the heat of the ovens. He dropped his hand. "Hey, I was just teasing. It's nice that someone cares enough to ask."

"Are you sure? I am nosy, and I can be so blunt sometimes."

"I like blunt. And I don't mind talking about things, when it's just you and me."

He watched as she relaxed. "Good. I don't make a habit of repeating all the intimate details of my friend's lives."

"Am I a friend?"

"You could be," she said, her honesty stirring up all sorts of forgotten sensations in his soul.

"I'd like that."

"You should know though, I've been warned away from you by just about everyone in town, except Dawn, the hopeful optimist, of course."

"I don't doubt that. Dawn seems sure of my redeeming qualities, but everyone else, well, let's just say the jury's still out."

"Should I heed those warnings?"

He thought about that a minute. "Probably, but I sure hope you don't."

"I told you—I don't judge people. I go with my instincts."

"Right, and what are your instincts telling you now?"

She cut out a few cookies with the precision of someone who'd done it time and time again. Jeremy carefully placed them on one of the baking sheets.

"They're telling me that you are a good man who got caught up in a bad situation. On the surface, nothing has changed. You're still that same man. And yet, for you, everything has changed."

He picked up a spatula to transfer cooled cookies from the pan to the counter. "Wow, you are a very wise woman. That just about sums it up."

She gave him an understanding smile. "I can't imagine what you've been going through." Then she shrugged. "All these years, you and I have lived in this area, with just a river separating us. Strange and amazing that now, we're suddenly thrown together, huh?"

"Strange, amazing and very pleasant," he said, shrugging right back at her. "Almost as if—"

"As if it was meant to be."

"Yes, I guess you could look at it that way."

"But you have doubts?"

"I'm thinking that Dawn made this happen. She seems to think we'd be good for each other. Of course, she's the only one around here who seems to think that."

She laughed, shaking her head. "Dawn is in love. Now she wants me to—"

She stopped, busied herself with rolling more dough.

"She wants you to be happy," Jeremy finished, not daring to voice what Gabi couldn't say either. Then he asked, "Well, are you happy?"

She turned to look up at him, her dark eyes reminding him of rich chocolate. "I'm content. I've settled into this routine, this way of life, that always puts my daughters first. I'd hate to mess with that."

"I understand."

She'd hate for *him* to mess with that, he guessed. "I need to find myself a nice routine again, but I'm not so sure I can go back to things the way they were before."

She gave him a thoughtful look. "You might have to change yourself, since you can't change the truth."

"What do you mean?"

"Well, you're home and everyone knows about you now. The hard part is over. Now you can start fresh, make a difference in your life. Reinvent yourself, so to speak."

He pressed his lips together. "I've never thought about it quite like that."

She cut out more cookies, her face furrowed. "I had to do that—change myself. I went from being a wife to being a single mother, a widow. I hated the way people stared at me and felt sorry for me. I decided I'd just have to deal with my life on my own terms. I'm trying to do that, to show my daughters a positive picture."

"What happened to your husband?" he asked.

The look she gave him made him wish he hadn't. Her eyes filled with a deep pain. "Could we not talk about it?"

"I'm sorry. Now *I'm* being nosy."

"It's okay. I just wouldn't want the girls to hear—"

"Okay, then let's talk about…our families. We both have big ones, we know that. Tell me all about yours."

"That could take all night," she said, smiling again. "Let me get these in the oven and I'll make us some coffee. Then we can take a little break."

He waited as she put the big tray in the steaming oven then poured fresh water into the coffeepot on the counter, admiring the way she moved around the kitchen with ease. Tonight, she wore her hair up in a haphazard ponytail. She had on a long, loose red sweatshirt with a goofy reindeer on the front, over worn jeans and sneakers. She was adorable. But she still looked worried and distracted. Wishing he hadn't brought up her husband, he decided to concentrate on the here and now. Nothing too personal.

"Okay, tell me everything about your childhood," he reminded her as she handed him a steaming cup of coffee.

She did, in vivid detail, her trace of an accent getting stronger as she regaled him with stories of growing up with one sister and four older brothers. Then Jeremy did the same, enjoying sharing childhood memories with someone who didn't question him or judge him. It made talking about his family much easier, and it also made him see that he really did miss his family.

"You know, we have enough material between us to start our own magazine," she teased.

"Not a bad idea."

She gave him a wide-eyed look. "Well, there you have it. You should try your hand at a family-type magazine. You know, something that deals with faith and family and how life throws us into crisis."

"But as Christians, we somehow overcome."

"Yes, exactly." She grinned. "We are so brilliant."

He had to admire her enthusiasm. "It's certainly something to consider."

"And I get a percentage of the profits, for helping you create it," she said, a serious look on her pretty face.

"Absolutely."

They worked on more cookies, the comfort of the quiet church settling over them.

"You asked how I'm doing," he said after a few minutes of silence. "I'm doing okay." He turned to take a patterned cookie cutter in his hand. "The holidays will be a real test."

"But you'll be with your family."

"Yes." He watched as she cut out a bell-shaped cookie, then he tried one of his own. "I suppose you'll do the same—dinner with the family, toys and gifts for the girls, the works."

She nodded, watching as he managed to mess up the cookie dough. "Here, let me show you."

She took his hand in hers, then placed his hand over the bell-shaped cookie cutter. "You have to press down in a clean cut, very quickly. Then you lift the dough up and put it onto the pan."

Jeremy enjoyed the warmth of her fingers on his. He made the cut, then took a spatula and placed the slightly misshapen design on the baking pan. "How's that?"

Gabi looked down at her hand, at the spot where their fingers had touched. "That looks good. You're a quick study."

"I'm learning something new every day, that's for sure. Especially since I've been around you." He held up his cookie cutter. "I guess I'm like this dough—I need shaping into something new and different."

She tilted her head. "We can't all be cut from the same mold. God didn't make us that way."

Her simple statement had a profound effect on Jeremy. "I'm going to remember that. Especially if you refuse to go out with me because you think we're so different."

She lowered her head, looking embarrassed. "What are you doing here tonight, anyway?"

She didn't want to look up at him. Maybe because she'd felt the same things he'd just felt: that tingling sensation in his fingers, that warmth, that nice soft fluttering inside his soul. Had she felt all of that, too?

He didn't push the issue, since he wasn't sure how

to handle things between them. "Again, you can thank your friend Dawn for that. More handiwork. I helped make the scenery for the Christmas play." He didn't add the part about working in the closed-up nursery and daycare. Let her be surprised that he'd been doing some very challenging painting.

She busied herself with rolling out more dough. "I guess that was fun."

"Yes, palm trees and camels, and the entire background for the stable scene."

She finally looked up, her dark eyes shining with enough light to rival any festive decorations. "The most important scene in the play. I'll be sure to look for your trademarks."

"I'm sure you'll spot them," he replied, wishing for things he had no business wishing for. "I probably missed some spots here and there."

"It's the thought that counts."

"Yes, I guess so." He finished his batch of cookies, making some tree-shaped and some shaped like Santa's boot. "Now I get to decorate cookies with you. What more could I ask for?"

Gabi started laughing. "We're some pair. Here on a Friday night, making cookies. What does that say about our social lives?"

Jeremy leaned close, smiled down at her. "Well, I don't know about you, but this is the highlight of my social calendar so far this season."

She got all flustered again. "You poor man."

"Not so poor," he said, his voice going low. "I get

to be with a pretty woman and I get to eat cookies. I do believe that's every boy's dream."

Gabi looked up at him, her eyes going wide. Thinking he'd gone too far in the flirting department, Jeremy said, "What's wrong?"

She lapsed into Spanish and pushed him out of the way, all fiery and flashing. "The cookies," she screamed, hurrying toward the oven.

The smoke-filled oven.

"We burned the cookies?" Jeremy asked, his voice echoing through the empty building.

"Yes," she said, grabbing the hot tray with two thick potholders. "Oh, I can't believe I let this happen."

"It was my fault," Jeremy said, taking the pan from her. "Can we make more?"

She sighed, then pushed at a strand of hair escaping around her temple. "I guess we'll have to. Hope you didn't have anywhere important to be tonight."

Jeremy grinned, then grabbed a burned cookie. "No place I'd rather be."

"You are trouble, you know that?" Gabi said, wagging a finger at him.

He bit into the too-crisp, too-hot cookie, then caught her finger in his hand. "I made you lose your concentration, right?"

"Right, because you distracted me."

"So…I'm a distraction. Is that good or bad?"

"I haven't decided yet," she retorted. Then she looked at his face and burst out laughing.

"What?" he said, laughing right along with her.

She reached up and brushed her fingers across his lips. "You have burned cookie crumbs all over—"

Jeremy grabbed her hand again, his tone soft and serious. "I *am* trouble, Gabi. You should know that, before things go any further."

She backed away, her laughter dying. "What things?"

"You and me, this friendship. I like being with you."

She turned away, working on creating more cookies. "Isn't that the way it should be, between friends?"

"Yes, but…what if I want more?"

She lowered her head. "What if I can't give more?"

Jeremy couldn't accept that, but he could see that she was just as unsure and frightened as he was right now. And she had been warned.

"I'll take what I can get," he said. "I could use a friend."

"Okay."

"Okay."

Then the doors burst open and the room was filled with the giggles and chatter of her two girls.

"We're here, Mommy," Talia said. "Hi, Mr. Jeremy."

"Hi, yourself. Ready to show me how to make these cookies look pretty?"

"You're going to help?" Veronica asked, her dark eyebrows lifting in disdain.

"If that's all right with you two," Jeremy said, amused and a bit scared all at the same time. He suddenly wanted to win over both these little girls.

"Whatever," Veronica said, tossing back her thick, dark hair.

"Whatever," Jeremy echoed, grinning over at Gabi.

They went back to the business of making cookies. For a few minutes, they were silent while the girls chattered and fussed. But every now and then, he'd glance up to find Gabi smiling over at him.

It was a start.

Is this how it started? Gabi wondered later as she got the girls ready for bed. Did falling in love begin with a little bit of a heartbeat and change into this neverending stream of awareness?

She tried to remember the first time she'd fallen in love. She and Octavio had been high-school sweethearts. She remembered being aware of him. He'd played football, so he was easy to notice. Big man on campus. The first time he'd looked at her, her heart had skipped a couple of beats. That had been a young, tender kind of love.

And it had ended on a horribly tragic note.

She didn't think she could bear that ever again.

After she'd kissed Talia good night—Talia always demanded a big hug and kiss—Gabi went into Roni's room to check on her.

"Whatcha doing, honey?" she asked, surprised to find Veronica sitting in the old wicker chair by the window.

Veronica sat with her legs curled up. "Nothing."

"Time for bed," Gabi said. She wouldn't get a hug

from her oldest. Roni was at the age where mushy stuff like that just wasn't cool. But she would be allowed to touch a hand to her daughter's long hair, and brush a quick kiss across her forehead.

"I'm not sleepy," Roni said, but she moved toward her frilly bed anyway.

"Is something wrong?" Gabi asked. Roni had been quiet on the way home.

"I don't know. Maybe."

Gabi waited until Roni was underneath the covers, then tucked the purple-and-pink flowered sheets and comforter around her daughter. She sat down on the side of the bed. "You know you can talk to me about anything, right?"

Roni gave her a long, appraising look. "Are you dating that man, Mama?"

Surprised, Gabi swallowed. "You mean Jeremy?"

Roni gave her an eye roll. "He's the only man I've ever seen you with besides Daddy."

That statement struck Gabi right in the center of her heart. She hadn't stopped to think what dating might do to her children. She hadn't been thinking straight at all.

Careful in how she handled this, Gabi took one of Roni's small hands in hers. "Honey, Jeremy is just a friend. It's okay for me to have friends who are men. You understand that, right?"

"I guess so," Roni said, her dark eyes wide. "It just…seems so…weird."

"But you seemed okay with it at Grandmama's

the other night. Why didn't you tell me you felt like this?"

"I don't always," Roni said. "I do like Mr. Jeremy. But I don't know if I want him around all the time. It just seems…different. He's not Daddy."

Gabi felt tears welling up in her eyes. "It seems that way to me, too. I loved your daddy so much. And it was very hard to lose him. But…it is nice to have someone to talk to."

"But you have people," Roni said, her tone high-pitched. "You have Grandma and Dawn and Aunt Yolanda. Can't you just talk to them?"

Gabi had to smile at that. "I *do* talk to them, honey. But…it's nice to have a…man to talk to."

"You were flirting," Roni said, her eyes accusing. "You like being with him, don't you?"

Gabi couldn't lie to her daughter. "I do enjoy talking to Jeremy, yes. And it's different, talking with him. We talk about all kinds of things—things that I can't talk about with my female friends. He's a nice man, Roni, but I don't want you to worry about anything. We're just friends."

Her daughter didn't look convinced. "I miss Daddy."

Gabi's heart went out to her daughter. Talia was younger, so she'd bounced back a lot quicker after Octavio's death. But Veronica was old enough to listen and understand that her father's death had come too soon. It was hard for her to grasp. It was hard for Gabi to grasp, too.

"I miss your daddy every day," Gabi said, pushing Roni's bangs away from her forehead. "But… missing him won't bring him back. I can't explain this very well, but I hope you will understand that one day I might date other men."

"I get it," Roni said, turning away. "You like Mr. Jeremy and you want me to like him, too."

"I'd like that, yes. Can you try, Roni? Can you give him a chance? You have to understand, he needs a friend right now, too. He wants to be your friend."

Roni didn't turn around. "Why does he need anyone? He has that big house and fancy cars."

"Even rich people have problems, honey. Money can't solve everything. And besides, I think Jeremy lives in a condo at the Enclave, not in the big house with his parents."

Roni turned back to her mother. "He's still got everything, so what's his problem, then?"

Gabi didn't want to go into that particular issue with her daughter. "Well, he got his feelings hurt. He quit his job and he went on a long trip. Now he's back and I think he wants…to start over. But he's afraid—"

"But he's—I mean, he doesn't look like he'd be afraid of anything to me."

"Looks can be very deceiving. He is a big, strong man and probably very brave. But inside, he's hurting and he needs to know that God loves him, that his family loves him. And he needs to know he has a friend—someone he can trust."

"So he picked you?"

Gabi nodded, smiled at the simplicity of that question. "Yes, he did. I can't turn my back on him. But…I can promise you this. From now on, I won't do anything without talking it over with you and Talia first. I should have explained things better to you. I'm just his friend right now."

"Right now," Roni repeated, her expression thoughtful. Then she sat up. "I'm sorry, Mama. I was just worried."

"You are too young to worry," Gabi said, wanting to hug her daughter tight and protect her from any worry or pain.

To her surprise, Roni reached out to her. Gabi pulled her daughter into her arms. "I love you so much."

"I love you, too," Roni said. Then she whispered, "Well, he does make you laugh. And…I like that. You're so pretty when you laugh."

Gabi blinked back tears. "Thank you, baby. Thank you so much."

After she said good night, Gabi went into her own room and sank down on the bed. She didn't know whether to laugh out loud now or burst into tears.

Jeremy Hamilton did make her laugh. He made her feel alive again. He gave her hope. But in spite of the way he made her feel, she wouldn't do anything to jeopardize the well-being of her children.

Dear Lord, what am I supposed to do?

She looked at her wedding picture there on the dresser, her silent prayers too hard to put into words.

She'd never before felt such intense pain and such sweet joy all at the same time.

In the end, the tears won out.

Gabi grabbed the empty pillow beside her own and cried herself to sleep.

Chapter Seven

A couple of days later, Jeremy parked his car in the lot next to Hamilton Media and headed toward the building, his steps a little more sure today. He grinned to himself, admiring the festive red bows tied around the street lamps and the two big evergreen wreaths hanging on either side of the doors. From a shop down the street, he could hear cheery Christmas music blasting from two speakers. Christmas was coming, and for some reason he was actually looking forward to the holidays. That dread he'd felt since coming home was slowly and surely changing into anticipation. A good kind of anticipation.

He supposed he had Gabi and her daughters to thank for his positive mood. He'd sure enjoyed helping them bake and decorate cookies Friday night. There was something to be said for simple tasks and simple pleasures.

Especially when those tasks and those pleasures were shared with a pretty, interesting woman.

They'd talked quietly about so many things—about their big families and the differences between the two, about Gabi's hopes for her girls, about his doubts for his future. And amid the talk, they'd laughed with the girls and made about six dozen beautiful, cheerful, slightly flawed cookies for some nice people who would appreciate their efforts.

Okay, steady, he told himself as he pushed through the revolving doors. *You don't need to rush into anything. Just...enjoy the moment.* That was something he'd never tried to do before. He'd always pushed ahead, to the next deadline, to the next big story, to the next issue.

But then, he reminded himself as he waved to Herman and Louise, he'd never had time before to be in the present. Hamilton Media demanded attention 24/7. This place had been his life, his only life. Maybe in a weird kind of way, there was a blessing behind all the pain he'd endured over the last few months. Meeting Gabi had helped to ease that pain and make him see things in a different way, especially about his own life and how he might need to make some changes. He liked the idea of starting a new magazine. The idea she had given him had him buzzing with new concepts and a new challenge. And for that, he was extremely grateful.

"Hello there, young fellow," Herman said, hurrying to hit the elevator button for Jeremy. "I can't tell you how good it is to see you back here."

"Hello, yourself, Herman," Jeremy said, leaning

over to shake Herman's gnarled hand. "It's good to be back, I think."

Herman nodded, then winked. "Can't keep a good man down."

Louise echoed, "Amen to that." Her smile was bright and reassuring as she held open her arms for a hug.

Jeremy welcomed her hug and the familiar scent of gardenias that always surrounded her. He held her with a new strength in his heart. "I've missed y'all."

The elevator door pinged open. Herman waved Jeremy inside. "Get on up there. They need you."

Thank goodness some things never changed, Jeremy thought as he waved to them and pushed the button on the elevator. He wanted to talk to Tim about his gut feelings regarding all this scandal. He couldn't dismiss Betty Owens in all of this. It made sense that she might at least know who was spreading these rumors. If he could get her to open up, he might be able to nip all of this in the bud before... before his father came home for the holidays.

Jeremy took a deep breath. He was beginning to cave regarding Wallace. He knew he wouldn't last much longer, wallowing in bitterness and anger. Wallace had been his father, in every way that mattered. And he didn't want Wallace to suffer because of all this gossip. So far, the family had been able to shield him from the worst of it. But Wallace's return home from the hospital would bring all kinds of visitors, good and bad, with all kinds of news, good and bad.

Jeremy's protective instincts kicked in with a fierceness he'd forgotten. His parents were getting older, and with his father being so ill, any extra stress would only add to their weariness and create more health issues for both of them. He wouldn't allow that.

Again, he silently thanked Gabi for this new state of mind. Who knew that baking cookies could change a man's whole perspective on life?

Who knew that being with a great woman could change a man so completely?

Then he got off the elevator and found his brother Tim leaning over Dawn's desk, grinning at her like a lovesick puppy.

Jeremy had to laugh. Who knew, indeed.

"Cut that out," he said as he approached the desk.

Tim jumped back, a guilty expression on his face until he saw it was Jeremy. "Oh, hi."

"Hi, yourself." Jeremy nodded to Dawn. "I never thought I'd see the day—my brother having an idle moment with a pretty woman. We're all so used to him barking orders, his fingers permanently attached to his PDA."

Tim shrugged, smiled down at Dawn. "What can I say? I'm in love. I have a different kind of PDA these days."

"Yes, public displays of affection. I never thought I'd see *that,* either," Jeremy replied with a smile. "But it's very nice to witness."

"You ought to try it yourself," Tim said, motioning Jeremy into his office. Then he turned to Dawn. "Lunch, right?"

"Yes, boss." She tilted her head toward Jeremy. "Want to join us?"

He shook his head. "I can tell my brother wants you all to himself. And besides, last time I went to lunch with you, it was clearly a setup."

"You didn't seem to mind."

"Not at all. I like Gabi."

Tim nudged him. "I've been hearing about this new development. So come on in and tell me all about it."

"Nothing to tell," Jeremy said, giving Dawn a meaningful look. "Even though some people would love for that to change."

Dawn only laughed. "Oh, I have a hunch it's going to change, in a very good way."

"Ever the optimist," Jeremy said, waving to her as he headed into Tim's office. He wasn't ready to admit that he really enjoyed being with Gabi. This town had enough gossip; he didn't need to add to the rumors by going on and on about how much he liked Gabi.

Tim waited until Jeremy shut the door, then pivoted to face him, his hands in the pockets of his expertly tailored wool trousers. "So, what's up with Gabi and you?"

Jeremy settled into a chair, then brushed his hands down his jeans. Maybe he could be honest with his brother, at least. "We're friends."

"Friends, huh? Interesting."

"Don't go analyzing this, brother. Gabi is a nice woman who feels sorry for me."

"Are you using that to your advantage?"

"That sounds like the old Tim."

"No, I meant it in the nicest kind of way. You need a good friend. Preferably someone who's not related to you." He looked down after saying that, then pulled his hand down his face. "I'm sorry. Touchy subject."

"We're still related," Jeremy said, surprised that the remark didn't sting as it would have a month ago. "Even if I don't want to claim you at times."

Tim sank down behind his desk, a wry expression on his face. "It's hard to imagine what you've been through. I don't know if I would have handled it any better."

"I'm getting better," Jeremy admitted. "And I do appreciate…your efforts toward helping me in that area."

Tim shrugged, shuffled through some papers. "You'll always be my brother."

Jeremy felt the sincerity of that statement deep inside his soul. "Let's not get all mushy. It'll ruin our images."

"Agreed. Now what's up?"

He shifted in his chair. "I think I might try to talk to Betty Owens about all these rumors. She seemed a bit standoffish when I went to lunch at the Bake Shoppe with Dawn and Gabi the other day. But then, when I think about it, Betty has always been a little closemouthed around me. I seem to bring out that quality in people."

Tim ignored the sarcasm and went right for the real issue. "Do you think Betty might be behind some of the leaks and rumors?"

Jeremy went to the credenza by the window and poured himself a cup of coffee, so used to doing this, he didn't even think about this being Tim's office now. "She does like to gossip, and she usually knows everything that's going on around here. It just makes sense—"

"That she might at least know who's doing this?"

"Yes. It won't hurt to start there, I think. I only hope she won't take it the wrong way, since one of the rumors suggested she might have had an affair with our father, and had a child from that affair."

"Surely you don't believe that?"

"I would have never believed Wallace wasn't my biological father, either, but that's the truth."

"Point taken. But…Betty and Dad? If it did happen, it had to have been right before he married Mother."

Jeremy took a sip of his coffee. "I agree, since Justine is about my age."

"Our dad was something, wasn't he?"

"Apparently he was a real ladies' man."

"Do you think—"

Jeremy frowned at his brother's obvious train of thought. "I believe he's been faithful to Mother, if that's what you're asking. His love and respect for her has always been very clear, and it's probably the most honest thing about him. I think he changed after they got married."

"He's still a hard man to understand at times," Tim said. "Even now, he'll argue with me about everything from politics to the lead story in the paper."

"Ah, I remember those days well," Jeremy retorted.

Tim got up to pace. "You need to be careful if you go to Betty, Jeremy. She might think you're accusing her."

"I'll handle it with kid gloves. I don't want to accuse anyone. I just want answers. And I want it to end. Dad will be coming home soon and I think this needs to be over, so we can have a fresh start for the new year."

Tim gave Jeremy a look filled with surprise. "You sound like a Hamilton again."

"I feel like a Hamilton again."

"Welcome back," Tim said, slapping Jeremy lightly on the back. "Does that mean you're ready to come back here to work, too?"

"Maybe." Jeremy finished his coffee. He didn't want to put a jinx on his magazine idea until he was sure, so he didn't mention it. For now, he was willing to help Tim out. "I suppose I could start by finding a new office, since you seem to have taken over this one completely."

"Do you mind?"

"No, and I want to make something very clear. You belong here, Tim. I can see that now. I don't mind one bit."

Tim looked shocked, then humbled. "Thanks, Jeremy. You know I'll do the job."

"I don't doubt that—just don't let the job do you in, like I almost did. But what can I do?"

Tim rubbed his jaw. "Well, if I'm the acting—or the new—CEO, and Amy is the senior managing editor of the magazine, how about we appoint you executive manager over the entire operation?"

"Is there such a position?"

"There is now."

"And what exactly would I manage?"

"You'd be good at organizing and updating the computer system and doing all the hundreds of things I don't have time to do. We need someone strong to rally the troops and…it would certainly free me up to concentrate on the actual meat of the paper. It would mean less of the creative side of things and more of the administrative, everyday operations around here. You'd be the glue that holds us all together, something that's been sorely missing since Dad got sick and you quit." He lowered his head, then added, "As you know, I'm not as much of a people person as you. People tend to run the other way when they see me coming. But you always had a way with the employees. I think you'd be great at keeping us all calm and focused. And that would free up Ed Bradshaw and allow him to get back to being the managing editor."

Jeremy looked out the window at a young mother pushing a baby stroller down by the river park, then he turned back to his brother. "I'd be more behind the scenes, right?"

Tim nodded. "Would you mind that?"

"No. In fact, I think I'd like that. I can take things slow and get back into the groove. And this would be a good front for me while I investigate all the past employee records, to try and find anyone who might have a grudge against us. But Tim, there's something you need to understand before we shake on this."

"Oh, and what's that?"

"This might not be permanent. I mean, I might want to move on to something else."

Tim looked puzzled at first. Jeremy imagined it was hard for his brother to grasp working anywhere but here. It was hard for him to grasp, too, and he hadn't realized until Gabi had put the thought in his head, that he might *want* to move on.

Tim let out a long breath. "Okay. Whatever you decide, you will always have a place here."

"Thanks." Jeremy headed for the door. "I'm going to talk to Betty. Then I'll come back and find an empty office around here somewhere."

"Sounds like a plan," Tim said. "You know, we never got anyone to replace Curtis. His office wasn't half-bad."

"Curtis Resnick?" Jeremy asked, his brow lifting. "Whatever happened to him, anyway?"

Tim frowned. "He's still in town, but he's keeping a low profile. I'm thankful I don't see him much."

Jeremy pushed away the guilt he felt each time he

thought about Curtis Resnick. He'd trusted the man and tried to give him a second chance after they'd discovered Curtis had been embezzling money from the company. Making that decision had been the beginning of Jeremy's downfall. "I thought he left."

"He should have. But he won't be bothering us anymore."

Jeremy remembered how his father and Tim had wanted to prosecute Resnick for embezzlement, but since he'd considered Curtis a friend, Jeremy had decided not to press charges. He only asked Resnick to pay restitution. He'd fired the man and warned him to stay away from Hamilton Media. They'd parted on good terms, considering everything that had happened. Apparently, Curtis had found other means of keeping up the lavish lifestyle he loved.

"Well, good riddance," Jeremy said, hoping he didn't run into Resnick any time soon. He still felt responsible for the man's crimes. Just one more bad decision for him to get over. "I could have handled that better."

"You were trying to be a friend," Tim said, no bitterness in his voice now. "I guess we have to remember that this is still a business after all."

"Yeah, and I have to be tough from now on."

"Then get at it, and I'll make the official announcement that you are the new…what did we decide to call you?"

Jeremy grinned. "Executive managing something something."

"Yeah, right, that." Tim laughed. "I'm teasing. I'll

put out the word and we'll have an official welcome-back party later this week."

"That would be nice. And in the meantime, I'll try to figure out what I'm supposed to be doing."

"You know the rule around here—if it needs to be done, just do it."

"Yeah, I think I came up with that rule."

"Well, we've stuck to it."

"Okay. See you later."

"Later," Tim said, rubbing his hands together. "Now I have lunch plans with a beautiful woman."

Jeremy chuckled. "I remember a time when you wouldn't even stop to eat lunch."

"Times have changed, brother," Tim said, walking him to the door. "Times have changed."

That sure was the truth, Jeremy thought as he left his brother and Dawn, then caught up with a few workers to quiz them about all these rumors. Unfortunately, no one could shed any light on the situation.

"I can't think of one person who's ever left here holding a grudge, Jeremy," Ed Bradshaw told him. "You were always very fair, even when you had to let someone go. Now, Tim, that's a different matter," he teased, grinning.

Jeremy thought about that, his mind going back to Curtis Resnick as he headed back down the elevator. The stipulation had been that Curtis would never speak to anyone regarding what had happened. And in return, Jeremy had put out a press release stating that Curtis had gotten a better offer and resigned.

Had Curtis broken that stipulation?

Jeremy decided he might need to investigate that angle, too. Then he thought about his life now that he was back. Everything had changed. His large family was growing with each new engagement announced and wedding planned. And to think, he was the oldest and still the least settled.

He thought about Gabi. Having met her, Jeremy decided settling down didn't seem so bad after all. He'd always put work ahead of his social life before, in spite of his mother's and sisters' efforts to introduce him to eligible single women all over Tennessee. He'd dated off and on, but most of the women who seemed attracted to him wanted either money or power or both, but never just him. And the very ones who'd been so set on being with him back then, wouldn't give him the time of day now that they knew the truth about him.

Gabi was different. She didn't seem all that impressed with money and she certainly didn't seem the type to be power-hungry. No, Gabi wasn't phony or presumptuous, and she didn't seem to have an agenda. Her whole background and upbringing was very different from his in some ways, and in other ways, very much the same. Her faith was strong, and because of that, Jeremy's own faith was slowly getting back to solid ground.

Jeremy decided he'd call her tonight, to tell her how much he'd enjoyed baking cookies with her and the girls. And maybe he'd ask her out on a real date. She'd probably turn him down flat, since she seemed afraid to take things any further between them. But it didn't hurt to ask.

Jeremy was so focused on his thoughts about Gabi that he almost ran into a woman coming out of Betty's. Holding up his hands to avoid knocking the woman down, he was surprised to see Ellen Manning, *Nashville Living's* former Makeover Maven, standing there, her designer purse held in front of her like a shield.

The stunning blonde looked flustered, her fair skin turning a bright pink. "Jeremy, hi."

"Hello, Ellen, how have you been?"

"I'm great. Just great. Got to go." She looked up and down the street, as if she was afraid she was being followed. "See you."

"Hey, wait a minute." Jeremy held her at arm's length. "I heard you'd left. It sure was sudden."

"No more sudden than your departure," she said, a fierce, daring look in her eyes.

"Touché," Jeremy said, dropping his hands. "I hope you're doing okay, Ellen. I mean that."

She glanced back over her shoulder, then bobbed her head. "I'm fine. Just busy."

"Okay. It was good to see you."

Jeremy watched as she hurried off and wondered if there was a fire somewhere. Ellen had always been a bit of a flirt, never missing an opportunity to chat it up. But she'd sure beaten a hasty retreat today. Maybe because she'd left Hamilton Media so suddenly and without a very good reason? Or maybe because she'd heard all about his paternity and didn't know how to respond to that?

Sighing, Jeremy supposed he'd just have to get used to people being uncomfortable around him. At least until this scandal died down. All the more reason to talk to Betty Owens. If anybody in this town might know who was spreading juicy tidbits about the Hamiltons, it should be Betty.

Jeremy opened the door to the Bake Shoppe and glanced around until he saw Betty behind the counter. She looked up at him, smiled, then went about her business. He'd just sit right up front until she was forced to speak to him.

Maybe, just maybe, he'd get some answers to help end all of this so his family could get back to normal.

Out in her sports car, Ellen Manning made a call on her cell phone, her hands shaking.

"Hi, it's me," she said, her voice just above a whisper.

"What's wrong?" the man on the other end of the line asked. "You don't sound so hot."

"I'm not feeling so hot. I just ran into Jeremy Hamilton."

"So? He can't hurt us now."

"He might be able to hurt us if he finds out what we've been up to."

"No way. We've covered our tracks on this, baby. You worry too much."

Ellen gazed around, making sure no one was

watching her. "I don't like all this secrecy. It doesn't feel right."

"Hey, the Hamiltons deserve everything they're getting. Or do I need to remind you of how you were treated when you worked for *Nashville Living?*"

"It wasn't that bad. Not like that dead-end job you talked me into."

"I told you, when this is all over, you can have any job you want, anywhere in the country."

"Well that can't be soon enough for me," Ellen said. "I've got to go. See you tonight?"

"Yeah, later."

She heard the phone click. He'd hung up. Just like that. No "I love you," no "Don't worry, I'm here for you." Not even any questions about how Jeremy had treated her when they'd run into each other. Thinking back, Ellen remembered she'd always had a thing for Jeremy. Only he'd been too much of a workaholic to notice. But he had treated her with kindness and respect, even when she'd gone to him ranting with all her problems. Which was a lot better than how her current man treated her, that was for sure.

Why did she always pick such losers?

Chapter Eight

"What can I do for you?"

Jeremy smiled up at Justine as she handed him a menu. "What's the special today?" he asked, scrutinizing her carefully. He tried to find something of Wallace in her, but he couldn't tell one way or another. Could this woman be the half sister of his siblings?

"Jeremy? The special—hamburger steak—do you want it?"

Jeremy shook his head to clear it, acutely aware that he'd been staring at Justine for a full minute. "Oh, I'm so sorry. Yes, that's fine. Did you get a new haircut?"

"No," she said as she fidgeted with the salt and pepper shakers on the counter. "Just a trim."

"That must be it. It looks nice."

"Thank you?" she said with a bit of a question at the end. "Now, would you like some lunch?"

Jeremy studied the menu. "Forget the special. I'll have a turkey club and a cup of coffee." Handing

Justine the menu back, he looked around then asked, "Where did your mom go? I need to ask her something."

Justine ran a hand down her apron. "Is it important? She's really busy in the kitchen."

"I won't take up much of her time. And yes, it's very important."

Justine glanced back toward the kitchen, her eyes wide with what Jeremy could only call apprehension. She hesitated, then said, "I'll see if she can come out."

His gut was telling him that these two had a secret, all right. But why would they want to spread all these rumors about his family—*if* they were the ones doing it? Then a thought formed in his head— if Justine was truly Wallace's child, maybe Betty had decided it was payback time. Could that be it? Now that Wallace had come clean about Jeremy's biological father, was Betty thinking it was time for Wallace to acknowledge Justine? Would she actually spread a rumor about her own daughter, just to get revenge on the Hamiltons?

He mulled that over while waiting, then decided it just didn't fit. Mainly because no one had actually said the supposedly illegitimate child might have been Justine. It had been implied, yet another part of the vicious rumor cycle. For all he knew, Betty herself didn't even know the article in the *Observer* had hinted at it being Justine. But then, how could she have missed it?

He looked up as Betty came out of the kitchen,

each of her steps slow and forced. Even her smile was forced. "Jeremy, is everything all right?"

"I'm not sure," he said, hoping he could keep his cool. "Betty, I need to ask you something and I hope you'll be honest with me."

She swallowed, pushed at her bun. The woman looked visibly shaken. "I'll try."

He took a long breath, glanced around to make sure no one was within earshot. "I guess you've heard all the rumors about my family, starting with me and working their way down. All these leaks—about Wallace not being my biological father, about Melissa's pregnancy, and…Well, there have been others—"

"What are you getting at, Jeremy?"

"I just need to know if anyone has been snooping around here, asking questions about my family?"

Betty let out a long sigh, almost as if she was relieved. "Oh, my goodness, Jeremy, you know people around here gossip all the time. I haven't heard any more than usual lately."

"Are you sure? I mean, it makes sense that you might hear things and…pass them on."

Betty stepped back, frowning. "I haven't contributed to any of the rumors about your family, if that's what you're implying. In fact, I've tried to defend all of you because of…well…your father being so sick."

Jeremy could tell he'd offended her. "Look, Betty, don't take this the wrong way. I just need information. If anyone has said anything to you, or asked you certain questions, I'd really like to know about it. I want all this scandal to be over when my father comes home for Christmas."

Betty leaned back against the counter. "I'll keep my ear to the ground, but honestly, I try not to put too much store into anything I hear. But you're right, I do hear just about everything. And I do like to chat with the customers. But I wouldn't do or say anything that might deliberately hurt someone. I hope you know that."

Jeremy nodded. "I'm not even suggesting that. I just thought maybe you might be able to shed some light on all of this."

"I'm sorry I can't help you more," Betty said, her mouth tightening into a solemn line.

Justine brought Jeremy's food, her gaze moving from her mother to him. "You two okay here?"

Jeremy nodded. "We're great." Then he looked back at Betty. "Thanks for talking to me."

"Any time," Betty said. Then she hurried away, her daughter trailing her.

Jeremy decided not to push the issue. But he was sure Betty and Justine were hiding something. Maybe they were just upset about the rumors of Justine's questionable paternity. Or maybe they didn't want anyone in Davis Landing to know that Wallace Hamilton might be Justine's biological father.

One way or another, this had to end.

He looked down at his sandwich, his appetite gone. Motioning to another waitress, Jeremy asked for a to-go bag, dropped some cash on the counter, then got up and left the restaurant.

In the kitchen, Justine turned to her mother. "He knows something, Mom."

"He was only asking about all the other rumors," Betty said, relief in her voice. "Not that."

"Still, he has to be curious. If he keeps poking around—"

"If they find out, we'll be just fine," Betty said. "We have nothing to be ashamed of. You just did what you had to do, honey."

"I know. But I don't want the Hamiltons to think the worst—that I had other motives for helping," Justine replied. "I just don't want any attention. I want to get on with my life."

"You'll be fine, honey," Betty said. "Just fine."

But Justine could see the worry in her mother's eyes.

"That pie sure was good," Gabi said, smiling over at Dawn. "I shouldn't have had it, though."

"One piece of pumpkin pie won't hurt you," Dawn replied, stirring cream into her coffee. "I think pumpkin's good for you, right? It's got lots of vitamins."

"Yeah, right," Gabi said, shaking her head. "I just won't eat much dinner."

Dawn relaxed back into her chair, her eyes scanning the sparse after-work crowd at Betty's. "It was a good idea to meet here. We can catch up. I've been so busy lately—"

"Tim is keeping you occupied?"

Dawn lowered her head, a soft smile on her face. "He sure is. But he knows I have to make time for my friends."

"That's good. He could be controlling, if you let him, I imagine."

"He's learning," Dawn said. "Now, what about you and Jeremy? Tell me about this cookie-baking session y'all had the other night."

Gabi looked out the window. Dusk was settling over Davis Landing. People hurried by, anxious to get home to the warmth of family and a home-cooked meal. She checked her watch. The girls were with their grandmother today, so they were safe. She looked back over at Dawn's expectant face. "It was nice. We had fun."

Dawn frowned. "*Nice* is good. *Fun* is good. So what's wrong?"

Gabi told her friend about Veronica's questions. "She's having a hard time seeing me with someone other than her daddy."

"That's tough," Dawn said, "but you have a right to some companionship, even if it's just friendship."

"I explained that to her. But now I'm having all these doubts."

Dawn leaned forward, compassion coloring her blue eyes. "Do you care about Jeremy?"

"I'm beginning to," Gabi admitted. "He's so…interesting, and he makes me laugh. But we're worlds apart. There's so much more than just a river separating us."

"But look at Tim and me," Dawn pointed out, her fork hitting her empty pie plate. "We came from very different backgrounds. Tim is rich, well-educated, Mr. Smart-and-Suave. Me, I'm just a working girl from Louisiana who had to find a job right out of high school. But we've worked through all of that. And he was great with my family when they came to visit for Thanksgiving. He and my brother Phil get along so well. You just never know how the Lord is going to pair you with a mate, Gabi. I mean, if we were all made the same, life would be pretty boring, right?"

Gabi had to agree with her friend's logic. "Well, Jeremy is certainly not like any other man I've ever known. He's exciting and, same as Tim, educated. He's a gentleman. He's so different from Octavio."

"Maybe that's what's bothering you the most," Dawn said. "That he *is* different from Octavio. Do you think you don't deserve someone like Jeremy?"

"Do I?" Gabi asked. "Look at me, Dawn. I'm Hispanic. I was married to a man I thought I'd spend the rest of my life with, a man who grew up with the same customs and traditions as me. I loved the life I had, and then something went terribly wrong. Now I'm not so sure where I belong, or if I'm supposed to have another man in my life at all."

"Then just take it slow," Dawn cautioned. "Does Jeremy know what happened with Octavio?"

Gabi shook her head. "No. He asked the other night, but I told him I didn't want to talk about it. I have to tell him sometime, though."

"The sooner the better. He'll understand what you've been going through."

"I just have to be very careful," Gabi said just as Betty came over with a steaming pot of coffee.

"Refill, ladies?"

Dawn nodded, then gave Betty a thoughtful look. "Hey, Betty, maybe you can help us settle an argument."

"I'll sure try," Betty said, careful as she poured them both a full cup of coffee. "What's the problem?"

Gabi was silent, but Dawn didn't hesitate. "Do you believe that two people from different backgrounds can't be happy together as a couple?"

Betty put the coffeepot on a nearby empty table then sank down in a chair next to Gabi and Dawn. "That's hard to say." She looked thoughtful for a minute, then glanced from Dawn back to Gabi. "I do think you have to tread very lightly in that area. Sometimes it's better not to mix things up too much. It can only lead to heartache."

"You really believe that?" Gabi asked, surprised that Betty seemed so adamant about this.

"I guess I do," Betty said, getting up. "Life is hard enough without having to deal with too many issues—there's those who have, and those who have not. That's just the way life is."

"But people are basically all the same," Dawn insisted. "We all just want to belong, to be loved, to have someone to love. I think love can overcome any obstacle."

"Honey, I wish that were true," Betty said, giving Dawn a sad smile. "But sometimes things just don't work out that way at all."

Gabi watched as Betty hustled away. "I guess that answers that."

Dawn shrugged. "I'm disappointed in Betty. She always struck me as more positive about things than that."

Gabi leaned close. "Maybe right now is not a good time to ask her about personal struggles. You know, what with that article that came out a while back in the *Observer*."

Dawn put a hand to her mouth. "Oh, I'd forgotten. But that's just talk. Betty was married to a good man. Not a hint of scandal."

Gabi nodded. "Exactly. But maybe she was thinking of what could have happened, if she'd gone in the other direction."

Dawn dropped her hands into her lap. "Oh, my." Then she tossed back her blond hair. "I'm not going to listen to rumors anymore. I refuse to. No matter what Betty thinks, I believe you should give Jeremy a chance."

"We're friends," Gabi said. "For now, that has to be enough."

"Just don't let this slip away," Dawn warned. "That would be a shame."

Gabi wondered about that. She didn't want to risk her heart or her girls' well-being just to explore the possibility of a future with a man from a different world.

And yet, as she sat here watching the sun set, she had to wonder if she'd regret *not* following her heart with Jeremy.

Jeremy sat in his condo at the Enclave, his gaze traveling over the familiar warmth of his home as he listened for Gabi's phone to ring. His apartment on the second floor wasn't as fancy as Tim's penthouse. But Jeremy liked the sleek dark wood of the built-in bookshelves nestled behind the brown leather sofa. He liked his recliner by the fireplace. And he especially liked the solitude of having a home office in the spare bedroom.

Only tonight, his haven felt lonely and way too quiet. Which was why he'd decided to call Gabi.

She answered on the third ring. "*Hola!*"

"*Hola,* yourself," Jeremy said, trying his best Spanish accent.

"Jeremy?" There was a minute of silence, then, "Oh, hello."

"Nice greeting, in any language," he replied, smiling.

"Thanks. How are you?"

"I'm fine. How was your day?"

He heard rustling and barking. "Busy. I'm putting away groceries. And Tramp wants a treat, as always. That dog seems to know whenever I go grocery shopping."

Laughing at the mutt's antics, he asked, "Want me to call back?"

"No, no. I've got all the frozen things put away.

Just a mountain of cereal and granola bars left to hide." Then he heard her talking to the dog. "Here, Tramp, here's your treat. Now go away." A pause, then, "Okay, I'm back."

"Okay." He leaned back, content just to hear her breathe. "I did call for a reason."

"Oh, and what's that? Got a hankering to bake more Christmas cookies?"

"Only if you help," he said. Then he added, "Actually, I thought I'd invite you and the girls to a tree-trimming party."

"That sounds like fun," she said. Then she became silent again. "Where is this party?"

"At my parents' house."

"Oh, I'm not so sure—"

"Tim suggested it. That brother of mine does come up with some good ideas now and then, but I have a feeling Dawn put the bug in his ear." He heard her sigh. Not a good sign. "Of course, I could be wrong there—"

"It was nice of Tim to think of us," Gabi said, "but I'd hate to impose."

Jeremy frowned, tried another tactic. "Look, Tim suggested this, but I'm the one inviting you. I'd love to have you there, Gabi. You'd really help me out."

"How's that?"

Sensing the doubt still in her voice, he said, "Well, everyone will be there with…someone. You know, my brothers and sisters have all gotten a case of the love-bug lately. I'll be the odd man out."

She laughed at that. "So this is a mercy date?"

"Yes, exactly. All you have to do is feel very sorry for me and say yes. I'll take care of the rest."

She went silent again. "And I can bring the girls?"

"Absolutely. What would a tree-trimming party be without children, anyway?"

"They might mess up your fancy tree."

"Never. This is always very laid-back and relaxed, especially this year. We don't want our mother going to too much trouble. We dress casual, eat way too much food, then we sing Christmas carols. That part is mandatory, by the way."

"I like to sing."

"Well, there you have it. I can't sing a note. You can help me out there, too."

"You're very pushy, Mr. Hamilton."

"I'm very needy right now." Did he sound too needy? he wondered, wincing.

"Well, since you put it that way…"

"Great, now you really do feel sorry for me."

"No, I think you're very humorous. But, this might be good for the girls. Holidays are hard— they miss their daddy."

Jeremy heard the hint of pain in her voice, and wondered if she was still mourning her husband, too. "I can certainly understand that. I hope this will cheer all of you up, and I know seeing y'all will make me smile. It's Thursday night. I'll pick you up."

"Okay." Then she said, "Jeremy, I don't really feel sorry for you."

"So that ploy didn't work?"

"No, not at all. But thanks for trying."

"Then why'd you say yes?"

Silence, then a long sigh. "Let's just say I'm willing to move out of my comfort zone. This get-together will be good for the girls, I think."

"I'm impressed," he said, "and hopeful."

"You haven't heard me sing yet."

"I can't wait."

They talked a few more minutes, then Jeremy hung up.

"I am needy," he said out loud.

But in his heart, he knew this need was different. He needed to be around Gabi. He needed to hear her laugh. He needed to draw strength from her smile and her faith.

"Is that so wrong, Lord?" he prayed out loud.

He walked to the window, looking out on the starlit night. He could see the Cumberland River glistening just beyond the trees, the nearby security lights hitting the water with a dancing clarity.

He wished things could be as clear with him. He was nervous about being with the whole family again at the tree party. But his mother would be disappointed if he didn't show up. At least Wallace wouldn't be there.

While Jeremy dreaded seeing his father again, he also prayed for his father, and for that dread to end. Maybe if he could solve all this scandal and put an end to it, he'd feel as if he'd accomplished something, but so far, he'd only reached one dead end after another on that. No one knew anything, or if they did, they weren't talking. And he hadn't been able to find out anything about his old friend, Curtis, either.

He'd keep praying. And he'd keep thinking about Gabi. Those two things should keep him focused and on track.

Chapter Nine

$\backsim$

Gabi glanced around, her gaze taking in the elegant, understated furnishings of the Hamilton mansion. She'd always wondered what this house looked like on the inside. But she'd never dreamed she might be standing here one day.

The central staircase looked like something out of a movie, while the big rooms on both sides of the entryway and long hall seemed to go on and on. She could probably fit her whole house inside the big room where everyone was gathering by the tree. The walls were covered with expensive artwork, the furniture was antique and gleaming, the chandeliers were glowing with muted, sparkling light. It was certainly not what she was used to. And she didn't plan on getting used to it, she told herself with a stubborn lift of her chin.

"How are you doing?" Jeremy asked as he handed her a glass of punch, his eyes questioning.

"I'm good," Gabi said, her nervousness sounding

in her low voice as she tried to wipe the defiance off her face. "The girls—"

"Are over by the piano with my mother, Amy's future stepson and Richard's nieces," Jeremy replied, a hand on her arm as he guided her from the central hallway to the two large parlors that had been thrown open for tonight's party. "They're fine."

Gabi could see that. Even Roni seemed to be having a good time tonight. She'd dressed both girls in bright Christmas colors, making sure that their hair was combed and their blouses and skirts were pressed and neat. She'd also fussed with her own appearance, hoping her discount-store Christmas dress wouldn't stand out in sharp contrast to the designer dresses of the Hamilton women.

As if he'd sensed her worries, Jeremy leaned close and said, "You look great, by the way. Green becomes you."

"This old thing," Gabi shot back, a bravado she didn't feel coming through her words. "I just pulled it right out of the closet."

"It's a pretty dress, so relax. No one is going to bring out the fashion police tonight."

"That's good to hear," she replied. "I just…I'm not used to fancy parties."

"This is *not* a fancy party," he told her, pulling her forward into the room full of people either standing or sitting everywhere. "I told you this is very informal."

"I can tell," she said. "That explains that table full

of wonderful food and all the glittering decorations and all the well-heeled people. I feel like tarnished tinsel."

Jeremy stopped just before they reached Chris and Felicity. "Hey, don't do that. Don't put yourself down."

Gabi felt embarrassed and ashamed. Why was she being so defensive? Because she knew she didn't belong here? "You're right. I sound like an ungrateful child."

"No, but you do sound like a woman who's not so sure of her own appeal. Trust me, this is not a tough crowd. As you well know, we all have our share of problems, too. And my sisters and brothers aren't going to judge you or tease you."

"No, because they have manners. And I think I need to remember that so do I," she replied. "Okay, no more doubts. I'm going to have fun tonight."

"That's better," he said, his smile full of encouragement. "Let's go talk to Chris. He's been waving at us for the past ten minutes. Then I have to take you to meet my mother. She's been asking about you ever since I told her I'd invited you and the girls."

Gabi laughed, then nodded. "I think I can handle that—I've actually spoken to your mother several times at the hospital, but only in passing."

Jeremy nodded, guiding her into the room. "You do have several friends here, too, remember?"

"So I do," Gabi said, waving to Felicity.

She could at least be herself with Felicity and their mutual friend, Stella Barton. Stella was Felicity's roommate and she also worked with Gabi at the hospital. So Gabi wasn't the only working woman here tonight. She glanced around, noticing Jason Welsh standing by the fireplace, deep in conversation with his boss at the police department, Lou Driscoll. All perfectly normal, average people, she told herself.

"Hi, you two," Felicity said as they approached. "Gabi, it's so good to see you here."

Gabi could sense the hidden question in that statement. Dawn had probably told Felicity she was trying to push Gabi and Jeremy together. "It's a nice party," Gabi said, careful that she didn't blurt out all her fears right then and there. "Where's Dawn, anyway?"

Felicity smiled, then pointed to a quiet corner of the big room. "Over there with the Typhoon. Although, I think Dawn has changed him into something a little more tolerable, like a lovely puff of wind."

"Amazing," Gabi said, noticing how happy Tim and Dawn looked as they whispered and laughed.

"A lot of people are hooking up around here," Felicity replied. Then she leaned close. "Tell me about you and Jeremy."

Gabi glanced over to where Jeremy stood talking to his brother. "Nothing much to tell. We met at church and we've been…getting acquainted. We're just friends."

"Oh, okay." Felicity didn't look convinced. "Well,

I'd say Jeremy thinks of you as more than just a friend. The man can't take his eyes off you."

Jeremy looked up then, smiling over at them, his gaze moving over Gabi with a warmth that rivaled the fire glowing in the big fireplace.

"See what I mean," Felicity said, grinning. "Love is certainly in the air."

Gabi was about to respond to that, when Jeremy walked toward them and grabbed her by the hand. "Come meet my mother."

She waved goodbye to Felicity and followed Jeremy to where Nora sat holding court on the piano stool, children at her feet. She looked like a perfect picture of a loving grandmother. That thought brought Gabi's heart to a lurching halt. What would it be like to have this classy, upper-crust woman as a grandmother to her girls?

Don't even think it, she silently told herself. *You've got to get out of this daydream and take a step back into reality. Your mother is a great grandmother.* But Octavio's parents had both passed away already. One more loving experience for her girls to miss out on.

"Mother, I want to introduce you to Gabriela Valencia," Jeremy said as he guided Gabi to Nora's side. "You've already met her daughters, Veronica and Talia, I believe."

The girls, sitting on low stools and munching on snacks from a big bowl on the table, grinned over at their mother.

Gabi sent them both a warning, motherly behave-yourselves-look, then turned back to Nora. "Hello."

Nora Hamilton looked up at Gabi, her expression full of interest. "Hello, there." She stood up, taking Gabi's hand in hers. "It's so good to meet you. Jeremy has told me so much about you. I'm glad he has you as a friend."

Touched and unsure how to respond, Gabi said, "It's very nice to meet you, Mrs. Hamilton."

"Call me Nora," Nora said, still patting Gabi's hand. Gabi felt the vein of strength inside the frail hand holding her own. "Call me Gabi, then," she said. Then she added, "I hear Mr. Hamilton will be coming home soon."

"Yes," Nora replied, her gaze moving to Jeremy's face. "We're all waiting for that day to come, I can tell you."

Jeremy looked uncomfortable, then said, "Mother, I've heard Gabi has a beautiful voice. Maybe you can convince her to sing a solo for us after we decorate the tree."

"I think I can do that," Nora said, pulling Gabi toward the piano. "What would you like to sing, Gabi?"

Gabi tried to pull back. "Oh, no. I couldn't—"

"How about I get things started?" Nora responded, a twinkle in her eyes. "Then after we've warmed up the crowd, you might be willing to pick a song, perhaps?"

Gabi could only nod, but she cast Jeremy a panicked glance. She didn't think she could sing a note in front of all these people.

He didn't offer her any way out. Instead, he just waved to her and watched as Nora literally took Gabi under her wing. They talked quietly for a few minutes, mostly about Gabi's girls and her work at the hospital and about Wallace's health and his homecoming. Gabi relaxed in spite of all her doubts. Nora was easy to talk to.

"It's time to get this big tree decorated," Nora finally said.

Gabi had to admit the giant blue spruce was beautiful, its fresh evergreen scent filling the room.

Nora clapped her hands to get everyone's attention. When that didn't work, Jeremy let out a shrill whistle, causing the children to laugh and the grown-ups to stop in mid-sentence.

"Hey, who's ready to decorate the tree? Because the sooner we get this tree trimmed, the sooner we can eat and sing."

Everyone clapped and started talking again. The children all ran toward the boxes of glittering decorations, ready to dig in. Jeremy moved a big ladder closer to the tree that shot up to the high ceiling. And then, they each started picking out decorations and either handing them up to Jeremy or hanging them on low branches. Some of the ornaments looked aged and faded, but Gabi could tell by the way the Hamilton siblings handled them that they all had special meaning.

She turned to find Nora looking intently up at the

tree, tears forming in her eyes. "Are you all right, Mrs. H—I mean, Nora?"

"I'm fine, dear," Nora replied, her hands touching on the pearls at her neck. "I'm just ready for my husband to be well and home. No one should have to be away from family during the holidays." Then she smiled up at Jeremy, her expression changing. "It's nice to see Jeremy having a good time for a change."

Gabi glanced up at him, too. "He was really looking forward to tonight. I'm glad I came."

"Me, too," Nora said, the sincerity in her eyes warming Gabi's heart and making her feel more relaxed. "I think your being here has helped him tremendously. I appreciate that."

Gabi looked around, thinking this family wasn't so different from her own. Loud, rowdy at times, subdued at others, but very close and loyal. She could understand why Jeremy needed a date tonight. Everyone here had someone special to hold close, someone to love. Ethan Dane held on to Heather, his hand occasionally touching her hair. They stood near Amy and her former college sweetheart and now-fiancé, Bryan Healey, who were sitting together hand-in-hand on a big ottoman. Richard McNeil hovered near Melissa, making sure she was comfortable. They were all here together, celebrating this joyous time of year.

It made her both happy and sad to be a part of the Hamiltons' celebration. But she wasn't sure how this was going to turn out, or if her life was going to be changed because of Jeremy. She could only dream of the kind of love many in this room had now. She'd believed she had that with Octavio, but maybe their love hadn't been strong enough. It certainly hadn't kept Octavio alive. And she wasn't so sure she could have that kind of love with Jeremy, no matter what her heart was telling her. She wasn't so sure she deserved a second chance.

Nora handed Gabi a glittering ball. "Go ahead, find your spot on the tree, Gabi."

Gabi smiled then handed the ornament up to Jeremy. He took it, his hand brushing her own. "Thank you."

Gabi understood he was thanking her for much more than just the ornament. "You're welcome."

The house was filled with laughter and chatter, everyone talking and vying for the best ornaments. In a matter of minutes, the huge tree glistened with everything from aged, handmade decorations saved from grammar-school days to new, glistening Christmas balls with this year's date on them. It was a lovely, heartwarming sight.

Jeremy's deep voice from high on the ladder brought Gabi out of her thoughts.

"It's good to have you all here tonight," he said, grinning down at them. "The view from here looks great, let me tell you." His warm gaze settled on Gabi. "Now it's time to put the star on top of the tree." He stopped, took a breath. "When we were little, our father always put the star on the tree. He's not able to be here tonight, so I guess I get the job."

He looked over at Tim. Gabi saw Tim's slight nod, then watched as Jeremy seemed to relax. "This year especially, the star we've had in our family for generations means so much to us. We've felt the prayers of everyone in this community. And we thank everyone for those prayers." He took the shining silver ornament and placed it at the very tip of the big tree, then laughed and bowed when everyone applauded. Then he called to Tim. "Brother, it's time to turn on the lights."

Tim went behind the tree and plugged in the cord. There was another sigh of appreciation and more clapping as white twinkling lights sparkled against the ornaments and branches of the tree.

"It's the most beautiful tree I've ever seen," Talia shouted out, causing everyone to laugh again.

Gabi watched as Nora hugged Talia close. "It sure is," Nora said, smiling down at Talia.

Touched, Gabi glanced back at Jeremy, her heart bursting with a new joy. The past few holidays had been full of sadness, in spite of her upbeat attitude with her girls. But tonight, Roni and Talia were smiling and truly happy. They basked in all the attention everyone here was showing them. Gabi thanked God for that.

Climbing down, Jeremy moved through the crowd to Gabi, his expression full of amusement and hope. "How'd I do?"

"You were…perfect," Gabi whispered. "The tree looks so pretty."

Jeremy seemed to breathe another sigh of relief. "I'm very glad you came tonight."

"Me, too."

Then he took her by the hand. "Let's find a private spot."

Wondering what was wrong, Gabi allowed him to pull her through the glowing house until they reached the darkened back corner of the long hallway, just inside the terrace doors.

"What's wrong?" she asked, all sorts of worries coursing through her. Had she done, said, something to upset him?

"Just this," he said. Then he pulled her close and kissed her.

Shocked at first, Gabi finally relaxed into the kiss. Jeremy's touch was warm and reassuring… and kissing him felt like coming home.

He raised his head, then pointed up over the door frame. "Mistletoe."

"Oh." It was the only word she could manage to say.

"'Oh' is right," he replied. "Let's just stand here all night."

"I think people would notice."

"In this crowd, I doubt it."

"The girls—"

"Right." He gave her a gentle peck on the lips, then tugged her back toward the front of the house. "This has been the best tree-trimming party of my life, by far."

Gabi had to laugh at his little-boy enthusiasm. "I'm glad you're having fun."

"Oh, it's only beginning," he said. "Remember after we eat, you promised me a song."

"I didn't exactly promise," she replied, panic once again whipping through her.

"But you will sing a song for me, right?"

"Only for you," she answered, against her better judgment.

"Only for me," he replied, clearly pleased. "Now let's go find some Christmas cookies."

She did sing, for the whole group. And she had a lovely voice. Jeremy listened as Gabi sang "What Child Is This?" with such a soulful, gentle rendering that he fell in love right there on the spot.

Amazing. In a crowded room, in his own home, with his family and friends gathered around, Jeremy had at last found the woman he'd been waiting for all of his life. He'd traveled across the South to find his grandparents, to find some sort of closure and understanding about himself and his birth, to find some part of himself in his biological father, only to come back home, still searching, still full of questions and bitterness.

And the very thing he'd needed the most had been right here all along. He supposed things did happen for a reason. Gabi was a widow now. And he had been lost in a vast wilderness of pain and longing.

But no more. *No more, Lord,* he thought, thanking God for the suffering that had brought him to this place. Jeremy gazed at Gabi as she sang, and felt the warmth of her charm and her practical nature covering him with hope and peace. But he also saw the veil of her doubt as she sang.

And he decided that, somehow, he had to overcome that doubt and make her his own. Somehow, they had to make this work. God hadn't brought him to this place, to this woman, only to abandon him, had He?

Show me the way, Lord. Show me the way. Jeremy kept that silent prayer in his heart as he listened to Gabi sing.

Chapter Ten

"Are you bringing someone to my wedding—a date maybe?"

Jeremy smiled over at his baby sister, Melissa. She'd come by his office at Hamilton Media, bringing pastries and coffee with her on her way to her own office.

Jeremy bit into a cheese Danish from Betty's and nodded. "I just might."

Melissa pushed back her long blond hair and placed a hand on her growing stomach. "Would that someone be Gabi Valencia?"

"I see the rumor mill is going strong," Jeremy answered. But for some reason, this particular rumor didn't bother him. He'd talked to Gabi on the phone several times since the tree-trimming party. Things were still unsettled and tentative between them, but at least she was willing to talk to him.

Melissa sank back in her chair and swung her booted foot. "Will you answer the question?"

"Okay, yes. I plan to ask Gabi to attend the wed-

ding with me. She seems to have a calming effect on
me, so I'm hoping that will make me behave myself.
I don't want to disgrace you on your big day."

Melissa kept patting her tummy. In spite of being
heavy with child, she was glowing with good health.
Jeremy had their family friend and lawyer, Richard
McNeil, to thank for Melissa's obvious happiness.
Although Richard was eleven years older than
Melissa, he'd had the same calming effect on her
that Gabi seemed to be providing for Jeremy now.

Melissa gave him a searching look. "You do seem
more relaxed, less panicked."

"So do you."

"Yes, I guess I am," she said. "I'm not even nervous about the wedding, since we decided to keep
things very low-key."

"You, low-key?" Jeremy had to laugh at that.
"What happened to that diva we all know and love?"

Melissa got up to gather their trash. "That diva is
about to be a mother. Kind of changed my perspective on things, know what I mean?"

"I think I do," Jeremy said, thinking about Gabi
and her girls. "I'm beginning to see that settling
down can change a whole lot in life. For the better."

"Then we've both reached the same place,"
Melissa said, her long peasant skirt fluttering around
her legs as she headed toward the door. She tugged
at the oversized blue sweater hanging down almost
to her knees. At the door she stopped, then turned
to come back to his desk.

"What?" Jeremy said, smiling up at her as she

reached down and hugged him tight. Touched, Jeremy held her close. "What was that for?"

"I love you," Melissa said. "And I'm glad you're home. I'm glad we're both home."

"Me, too," he replied. "We're going to get through this, all of this, together."

Melissa straightened, blinked back tears. "I didn't get a chance to talk to Gabi the other night, but she seems nice. She's very exotic."

"Yes, and very pretty."

"You're smitten."

"I think I might be. But there are still some hurdles to overcome."

Melissa tapped her tummy again. "Then you have to find a way around them. I did."

Jeremy leaned back in his chair. "You stood up to Wallace. I'm impressed."

"It wasn't easy, but I think I grew up that day. I realized I have to be responsible for my mistakes. And I also realized how blessed I am, to have a family like ours."

"I get you," Jeremy replied. "I've never doubted that."

"Then maybe it's time you paid Daddy a visit yourself."

"Maybe." He waved her out the door, then sat staring down at his desk pad. He couldn't put off seeing his father much longer, but each time he thought about confronting Wallace, that same deep dread filled his mind.

All the more reason to invite Gabi to Melissa

and Richard's wedding with him. Wallace would be there. And Jeremy wouldn't cause a scene at his sister's wedding. If he had Gabi with him, he'd be so distracted by her smiling face and practical humor, he just might make it through the day without a confrontation.

He was just about to call her at work when the door to his office burst open and Heather rushed in.

"Hi," she said, breathless, "I need your help down in personnel."

"What's the problem?" Jeremy said, always happy to see yet another of his sisters—this one feminine and shy, but still full of dynamite, nonetheless.

"Oh, just a glitch in the computer system. Tim was all tied up with an editorial meeting and Amy's at the hospital visiting Dad, and it seems everyone else is either busy or not responding to my pages. We might need to call a tech, but I thought you might want to check it first. Can you help me?"

"Of course," Jeremy said, glad to be back in the swing of things. "That's why I get the big bucks."

Heather shot him an impish look. "I'm so glad you're back. We need every able body around here. And with the wedding coming up, the holidays around the corner, and Dad coming home, well, I can only handle so much."

Jeremy gave her a quick peck on the forehead. "Not to mention you have a life now—with Ethan."

"Yes, I certainly do," she said, grinning as she hurried him out the door. "But I hear I'm not the only one with a new social life."

Jeremy grinned, shrugged. "What can I say? If you can't beat 'em, join 'em."

"You just didn't want to be left out of things, right?"

"Right. I'm jealous of all of you."

Heather took him down a long hallway to personnel. "It is pretty amazing, how we've all found significant others."

"Yes, it is. I guess everything happens for a reason."

"Do you really believe that?"

"I think I do."

"Then you should go and see Dad."

Jeremy winced. "You are the second sister to tell me that today."

Heather pushed at a big door leading into the computer room. "We just want things to be back… the way they used to be."

Jeremy didn't have time to respond to that remark, but he wondered if things would ever be the same again. He definitely knew that he was running out of excuses. He'd busied himself here at work, discreetly trying to investigate whoever had betrayed his family, and his after-hours were taken up painting at the church. What little free time he had, he either went jogging in Sugar Tree Park, or called Gabi. But, sooner or later, he was going to have to deal with his father.

Gabi looked up at the clock. Thank goodness it was time to go home. Her day at work had been non-stop and in crisis mode, it seemed. The phone had rung incessantly and she had a ton of data entry to get recorded before the end of the year. But right now, she had to get home to finish working on the girls' costumes and make sure they got their dinner on time for a change.

"Hey, ready to go home?"

Gabi looked up from turning off her computer to find her friend Stella Barton standing there with a thick file in her arms.

"Most definitely. What a day."

"Tell me about it," Stella replied, tugging at her hair. "The holiday flurry, as usual."

"And I've still got so much to do," Gabi said as she gathered her things. "My mom's helping make the costumes for the girls. You know, for the play at church."

"Oh, right." Stella walked alongside her as they headed out to the parking lot. A tall, blond man held the door for them. Automatically thanking him, Stella glanced back, then continued, "That's next week, right?"

"Right," Gabi said, wondering why the tall man looked so familiar, "and Roni and Talia are so full of pent-up energy it's about to do me in."

"You'll survive," Stella said, laughing. "You always do." Then she turned as they reached their cars. "How are you holding up, anyway?"

Gabi knew what her friend was asking. Stella wanted to know how the grief process was going. "It's still hard. One day I'm fine, the next day, I can't stop crying. I don't know if I'll ever get over it completely."

"Have you talked to Reverend Abernathy?"

"Oh, yes. And he's been a great comfort. He tells me just to go with it, not to try and fight it."

"Probably good advice."

"He also tells me to keep busy, to reach out to others."

"You've always done that," Stella said. Then she tilted her head and grinned. "But I hear that reaching out has gone beyond immediate family and friends."

Gabi sighed, threw her things into her car. "I've told you all about that already."

"Yes, you've mentioned Jeremy Hamilton a couple of times in passing. But the other night—"

"You were surprised to see me with him at the family compound?"

"Yes," Stella said, giving her a thumbs-up. "Surprised, but pleased. We're all rooting for you."

Gabi nodded, zipped her jacket closed. "I'm not so sure anyone should be holding their breath. Jeremy and I are just—"

"Friends, I know, I know," Stella said, finally opening her car door. "Friends from two different worlds, with the odds against them, right?"

"Right."

Stella got into her car, then looked up at Gabi. "You can't fool me, Gabi. Even though you're having bad days, I've seen you smiling a lot more lately. And if Jeremy is causing that, then I say more power to the man."

Gabi waved as her friend shut the door and drove away. With a groan, Gabi got into her own car and shut the door. She sat there, her hands on the steering wheel, wondering how she'd possibly thought her friendship with Jeremy could remain private and just between the two of them. Maybe that good-looking man they'd just encountered at the doorway to the hospital had heard things, too. She wouldn't doubt it, the way he'd scrutinized Stella and her. Was she destined to go around from now on wondering if people were gossiping about her?

"It's a small community, Gabi," she told herself as she made a face in the rearview mirror. On one level, she understood everyone's concerns and suggestions. Most of her friends were sincerely hoping things would work out for Jeremy and her. But she'd sensed other things couched inside their encouragement—worry, doubt, fear and maybe...a way of trying to protect her. It was sweet and endearing, but Gabi wished everyone would just trust her and let her get through this on her own.

With God's help.

She closed her eyes, the beginnings of dusk settling around her like a golden blanket. "Lord, I need Your guidance. I need to find a way. I want to be happy, but I don't want to ruin things for my children. I need You, Lord."

The short prayer brought her a brief sense of peace, but Gabi knew that the more she saw Jeremy, the more complicated things would become. Would she have the courage to keep things in perspective and consider him a good friend, or should she just end things now, before they both got hurt?

She watched the December sun set over the Cumberland River and knew in her heart that she didn't want to end things with Jeremy. But she was so afraid to take that next step, too.

Well, she certainly didn't need to sit here wasting time on it, that was for sure. Cranking her cantankerous economy van, Gabi backed up, checking the rearview mirror to make sure no other cars were coming.

That's when she saw the well-dressed blond man again. He was strolling through the parking lot, a newspaper in his hand, but he seemed to be watching her as she pulled away.

Gabi felt a chill go down her spine, then quickly pushed her uneasiness away. She'd seen that man before. He was probably just visiting someone in the hospital, and she'd probably passed him in the hallways. That had to be it.

As she drove by, the man stood on the sidewalk staring at her, his expression a cross between smug and sinister.

And Gabi had to wonder why he kept watching *her*.

Two hours later, Gabi sat on the couch, stitching away at Talia's angel costume. "Almost done, honey," she told her youngest.

"I can't wait to try it on," Talia said. "*Abuela* did a good job, didn't she, Mommy?"

"She sure did," Gabi agreed. "She only left the easy parts for me, bless her."

Talia lay curled on the floor, reading over her English homework. Roni was in her room, supposedly finishing her own lessons. But Gabi was sure she'd heard a radio blaring from that part of the house. She was worried about her oldest. One minute, Roni was bubbly and all girl, the next pouty and way too serious for a ten-year-old. All the more reason to take things slow with Jeremy. Her girls had already suffered enough confusion and heartache to last them a lifetime.

But she intended to protect them and give them the best life possible. Which was why she had tried to talk to them about Jeremy, and always included them in her decisions regarding Jeremy. Talia seemed fine with it, but Roni waffled back and forth. Gabi couldn't be sure how Roni really felt.

Gabi glanced around, remembering happier times when Octavio sat in the chair across from her, watching television. Her heart ached with longing. She wished she could find a way to get past this last hurdle of depression. She chalked it up to meeting Jeremy, a man who had all the material things Octavio had always dreamed of giving his family. Her husband had tried so hard, and because he thought he'd failed, he'd gone through his own dark torment.

Gabi couldn't think past that, so she put thoughts of their last days together out of her mind, forcing away the bitter memories. Instead, she concentrated on the here and now. But comparisons of Jeremy's life with her own kept making her feel edgy and full of doubts.

She was secure and warm, her daughters were safe, happy and loved. She had a good job and she had her friends and family. It would have to be enough.

She needed to put thoughts of the other man now in her life, this one rich and powerful and handsome, out of her mind. She was much too practical for daydreams. Jeremy was not a dream; he was a reality. He had problems and issues, just as she did. It didn't really matter that he had a vast amount of wealth. He was still hurting, still confused. She didn't know if she could offer him anything more than friendship.

Friend, she thought. *I can be his friend. Nothing more.*

The phone on the table beside Gabi rang. Putting down her needle and thread, she grabbed the receiver. "*Hola?*"

"I love the way you say that."

"Jeremy, hi," she said, her voice going low. So much for putting him out of her mind.

Talia rolled over, grinning up at her.

"How are you?" he asked, the intimate tone indicating that they were much more than just friends now.

"I'm okay. Stitching angel wings right now."

"I didn't know you had another part-time job."

She laughed at that one. "No, no Higher Source has hired me for my sewing services. It's just a costume for the church Christmas play."

"Oh, yes. That play has kept me pretty busy, too."

"It should be a big success," she said, hoping he'd come to watch the girls. But she didn't voice that hope. "That is, if I can just get these costumes finished in time."

"Didn't you tell me you enjoy sewing?" he asked.

"Yes, I did. I mean, I do, under normal circumstances. But I've been so busy lately, I had to get my mother to help out this time. She's been sewing clothes for most of her life. She made a lot of my school clothes."

Silence followed. That comment sure highlighted the differences in their lifestyles. Jeremy probably had his suits tailor-made in Nashville.

"Uh, I need to ask you something," Jeremy finally said.

Wondering what he was thinking, Gabi said, "Okay."

"Would you go to Melissa's wedding with me? I know we mentioned it that day we had lunch a while back, but I'd really like you to go with me."

Gabi's silence filled the phone line. Should she just tell him no and get it over with? She almost did, but his next words stopped her.

"I'd really appreciate it," he said. "My father will be there. It's going to be hard…seeing him again."

"How can I help?" she heard herself asking.

"Just by being there. You...seem to make me behave."

"I do?" She had to smile at that. "How do I do that?"

"Like I said, by just being there. When I'm with you, things don't seem so bleak."

Gabi held the white satin and netting of the costume in her lap, her heart fluttering just like these tiny wings. Jeremy had summed up their time together in a nutshell. When she was with him, things didn't seem nearly so bleak.

How could she turn him down, when she needed the same things he did? She needed to be away from the pain of her grief, if only for a few hours.

And, she needed to help him, as a friend.

"Will you go?" he asked, sounding unsure and unsteady.

"Hold on," she told him. Putting down the phone, she motioned to Talia. Together, they went down the hall to Roni's room. Gabi knocked on the door, then went inside the tiny room, Talia's hand in hers.

"What's wrong?" Roni asked, coming up off her bed where she lay doing homework.

"Jeremy is on the phone," Gabi explained. "He wants me to attend a wedding with him. His sister is getting married and he's nervous about being with his entire family again." She took a deep breath. "What do you two think about it?"

"You should go, Mommy," Talia said with a snaggle-toothed grin. "Weddings are so pretty."

Roni rolled over to stare up at the ceiling.

"Roni?"

Gabi waited, wondering if she'd be able to tell Jeremy she couldn't come. She would, if Roni seemed upset.

Roni finally lifted up to a sitting position. "I think that would be cool, Mommy."

"Really?"

Roni bobbed her head. "Will Sonia stay with us? And can we order pizza and watch a movie?"

Gabi let out the breath she'd been holding. "I think I can arrange that. I might even make you homemade lasagna."

"Even better," Talia said.

Gabi hurried back up to the den. "Jeremy, are you still there?"

"I am," he said. "Is everything okay?"

"Yes, I just had to clear this with the girls."

"Oh, I see. And what did the girls say?"

"They seem to think it's a good idea."

"Whew, I'm glad to hear that. But what about their mother? I mean, do you really want to go with me?"

"Of course," she replied, all the warnings and arguments inside her head subsiding for now. "How can I say no, since Dawn keeps insisting I should, and now you've asked so nicely. Even the girls think I should. And it would be rude to turn you down."

She heard his sigh of relief. "Thanks."

"Is this a fancy wedding?" she asked, once again acutely aware of their different backgrounds.

"Very simple, ceremony at the church, reception in the fellowship hall."

"Okay."

"Are you all right with this—being my date again? Do you still feel sorry for me?"

"That excuse is wearing very thin."

"That's what I thought. Does this mean you actually enjoy being with me then?"

"I admire you," she said, meaning it. "And, yes, I do enjoy being with you."

"I feel the same," he replied. Then he hesitated, "Gabi, listen. You do mean a lot to me. I hope you know that."

She sat very still, her pulse shooting through her with little electric shocks.

"Gabi?"

"I'm here."

"After the holidays, can we end the mercy dates and just…get to know each other better?"

She wanted to say yes, but a solid wall of fear caused her to hold back. "Let's just get through the wedding and we'll have to see."

"I guess I'll have to settle for that," he answered. "For now."

Gabi hung up, that "For now" ringing sure and clear in her head. Jeremy wasn't the kind of man to give up so easily.

And she wasn't the kind of woman to hold out forever.

She looked down at the silver garland shining so brightly in her lap, her hand touching on the shimmer of the gossamer wings as she thought about her fragile heart. Then she asked God to lift her up on angel wings, and help her find the light of hope once again.

Chapter Eleven

Gabi stood in the middle of her tiny den, her heart beating with each blink of the lights on the Christmas tree.

"Mommy, you look beautiful," Talia said, accenting the word *beautiful* with exaggerated excitement.

"Do I?" Gabi asked, checking her hair one more time in the mirror on the wall by the door. Her sister Yolanda had helped her coax it into a cascading up-swept style, with soft curls falling down around her face and neck.

"You do, honestly," Roni said, her big brown eyes going wide. "That dress must have cost a lot of money."

"Not really," Gabi said. "I found it on a clearance rack at Engel's. It had to be altered, but your *abuela* helped with that."

She swept a shaky hand over the peach-colored chiffon. The dress had been tossed to the back of a big sale rack. It was wrinkled and ugly-looking on the rack, but Gabi had seen the seventy-five-percent markdown and decided she'd have to make it work. It looked much better on than it did on the rack. With her mother's help, she'd worked on making it fit. The scooped neck wasn't too low, and the long chiffon sleeves now clung to her arms with a sheer shimmering perfection. The full skirt flared out in soft folds that fell down past her knees. She'd put on her good black pumps and Dawn had loaned her a glittering beaded evening bag. Her mother had loaned her a set of pearls and the earrings to match.

"Will I do?" she asked the girls.

They giggled and nodded. "Mr. Jeremy is going to love this," Roni said, grinning.

Glad that Roni seemed to be coming around as far as Jeremy was concerned, Gabi breathed a sigh of relief. "I just don't want to embarrass him. I want to look nice for this wedding."

"He won't be embarrassed," Talia said, her little hands on her hips, her denim pleated skirt fluttering as she swung back and forth. "He's gonna be proud."

The doorbell rang, causing Gabi and the girls to squeal in anticipation. "Sonia, I'm leaving now," Gabi called to her niece. Sonia was on the phone with a friend. "It's duty time."

"Coming," Sonia called. Gabi heard the click of the phone in her bedroom. "Sorry, Aunt Gabi—" She stopped as she hurried up the hallway. "Wow."

Roni had just opened the door and Jeremy stood there, echoing Sonia's one word. "Wow."

Gabi blushed as he looked her over with an appreciative smile. "Wow," he repeated, his smile beaming.

"Hey, that's my word," Sonia said, a teasing light in her eyes. "Doesn't she look fabulous?"

"Fabulous," Jeremy said. Then he laughed. "I sound like a parrot."

That made the girls giggle.

"You look nice, too, Mr. Jeremy," Talia said.

Jeremy tugged at his dark bowtie. "Do I?"

"Yes, you do," Gabi said, her words low. "Are you ready to go?"

"I think so. I am now, at least." He turned to face the girls. "I promise I'll take care of her."

"Don't be late," Roni warned. But her smile was full of hope.

Gabi felt the brilliance of that hope inside her heart, but she pushed the light away. She had to remember this was just a night out at a wedding. A night where she could pretend that she was someone she wasn't.

"You do look great," Jeremy said as he helped her into her black wool coat.

Gabi kissed the girls good night and reminded Sonia about the lasagna in the oven. Then she went out the door, Jeremy's hand touching her back as he guided her to his sleek sedan.

"It's been a while since I've gotten all dressed up," she admitted.

"This won't be so bad," he said, as if reading her mind. "Very simple."

"But still very Hamilton."

He gave her a puzzled look. "Whatever that means."

"I'm sorry," she replied as she settled in beside him. "I'm just a little nervous."

"That makes two of us."

Feeling worse because of what she'd said, Gabi turned to face him. His jaw was set in stone, as if he had willed himself to do this. And here she was, making light of his family and his status.

"Are you all right, Jeremy?"

"I think so. I don't normally sweat before a family function, but so much has changed. Melissa is pregnant by one man and getting married to another. The whole world has shifted since my father got sick. I just need to find my balance again."

Gabi couldn't stop herself. She reached out, taking his hand in her own. "I'm glad we found each other. I want you to know that."

He seemed to relax then. "What a relief. I was afraid I was torturing you, making you babysit me at another family event."

"You're too old to have a babysitter. But I am your friend."

"Oh, we're back to that again." He kissed her hand, then turned to crank the car. "I'm going to have to work on changing your mind about that."

Gabi felt the warmth of his kiss on her fingers. He wouldn't have to work too hard. She was beginning to care about him. She was beginning to think beyond reality and more into daydreams.

And that was dangerous territory.

* * *

Jeremy watched as his sister kissed her new husband. Then Reverend Abernathy announced the couple as Mr. and Mrs. Richard McNeil and everyone clapped and cheered. Melissa looked radiant and happy. She wore a demure cream-colored gown that flared out around her. Richard wore a dark suit and a huge grin.

"They're really in love," Jeremy said to Gabi, whispering the words with awe in his voice.

"I can see that," Gabi replied, tears in her eyes.

"Do weddings make you cry?" he teased.

"I was just remembering," she said. Then she shook her head. "I'll be okay."

Jeremy waited until the bride and groom had left for the reception in the fellowship hall, then turned to Gabi. "I guess this does bring back memories for you."

She nodded. "Octavio and I got married here."

They headed out a side door of the church. "That's the first time you've ever mentioned him."

"I don't like to talk about it."

Jeremy wondered if she was still in love with her husband. Was that why she was being so distant with him? Did her heart belong to someone else, someone who would never come back to her?

When they got outside, Gabi held her arms close around her. "It's getting cold."

Jeremy tugged her into the hallway leading to the education buildings of the church. "Before we go into the reception, I want to show you something."

She looked puzzled, but followed him as he guided her into the dark wing that housed the nursery and daycare center. "We're not painting tonight, Jeremy."

"No, we won't have to." He flicked on the lights. "I finished it this afternoon."

Gabi gasped, her gaze taking in the walls all around the long room. "Jeremy, did you do all of this?"

He grinned, nodded. "I did. I purposely asked the education director to keep it a secret until I was finished."

She whirled around, her peach-colored dress floating out like clouds at sunset. Jeremy had to find his breath. "That explains why Mrs. Grisham keeps shooing me away each time I tried to come in here."

"I hope the wait was worth it," he said, proud of his handiwork. "The kids have been temporarily displaced to some rooms down the hall, but this Sunday they get to see their new childcare center."

He watched as she lifted her brows, a surprised expression on her face. "You painted Noah's Ark all by yourself?"

"I did." He couldn't stop grinning. "Mrs. Grisham convinced me that I was the perfect man for the job. And then the good reverend backed her up and Dawn got in on the act and well...I painted Noah's Ark all by myself."

He was hoping she'd be pleased. He was not prepared for her tears. "Gabi?"

She looked down, holding a hand to her face. "It's just…that…this is the sweetest thing."

Jeremy's heart melted as he rushed to her and took her into his arms. "Does it look that bad, sweetheart?"

"No," she said, laughing now. "It's hard to explain."

Jeremy tried to understand. He held her close and glanced around at the wall behind them, remembering how he'd struggled with drawing the pattern on that wall, how he'd obsessed every other night when he'd come here after work at Hamilton Media, making sure the giraffes looked like giraffes and the elephants had the proper size trunks. He'd even managed to get the tiny mouse in the corner just right, according to the massive stencil Mrs. Grisham had provided him with. Now he wondered why Gabi was crying.

"Are you happy, at least?"

"Very."

"But you seem so upset."

She pulled back, wiping tears away. "I always wanted Octavio to do this. When the girls were little, he promised me. He promised me." She started crying again. "He never got the chance."

Jeremy's heart accelerated to a fast-paced cadence. "I'm sorry. I didn't mean—"

She touched a hand to his mouth. "Don't apologize. I love it. I love it. It's the sweetest, nicest thing you could have done for this church and for me."

He stepped back, afraid to voice what was in his

mind. "But…you wish your husband was here, you wish he'd been the one. You're still in love with your husband."

She looked surprised, then ashamed. "I want to still be in love with him. It doesn't seem right, being here with you. I should honor him. I should remember him."

"You can still do that, but you also need to remember that you're still alive, Gabi." He touched a hand to her arm. "And I'm here. I'm right here."

She looked up at him then, her big brown eyes going wide with hope and with admiration. "And you painted Noah's Ark."

"Yes, I did. For you."

She rushed into his arms and kissed him. "Thank you."

"You're very welcome."

Jeremy stood and watched as she danced around the room like a ballerina on a stage. He had to swallow the lump growing in his throat. He was in love with Gabi.

But he still had to compete with her late husband.

Once they were inside the reception hall, Jeremy spotted his parents sitting at a round table in the corner. He'd managed to avoid Wallace before the wedding. Things had been too hectic, but now he was running out of reasons and places to hide.

Earlier, he'd watched as his proud, determined father had escorted his sister down the aisle toward her waiting groom. Wallace's steps had been slow but sure, his head held high as he gave Melissa away. Even though the entire family had argued and bickered that he shouldn't make the short walk, Wallace wouldn't hear of it.

"She's my daughter and I'm fit enough to give her away," Wallace had told Nora. Jeremy had been in earshot of that conversation, but he hadn't stepped forward to contribute to the argument. He'd stayed in the background, Gabi by his side.

Now his father looked tired, his smile strained as he leaned forward in his chair, one hand patting his wife's arm. Nora Hamilton was dressed in a baby-blue wool suit, while his father had chosen a debonair gray suit. They looked the perfect picture of the proud parents of the bride.

"Are you going to stand here all day, or go over there and talk to Dad?"

Jeremy turned to find Chris giving him a daring look. "I'm not sure what I'm going to do."

"He's been asking for you," Chris replied, his brown eyes full of a stubborn glint. "Just say hello to him, Jeremy. What can that hurt?"

Jeremy thought about that, deciding it could hurt *him* a lot. Would his father acknowledge him, or reject him again right there on the spot? He glanced around, looking for Gabi. She was laughing and chatting with Amy and Heather.

Chris nudged him. "She's a nice woman."

Jeremy gave his baby brother a wry smile. "You say that as if to remind me not to mess things up with her."

"Did it come out that way?" Chris shrugged. "Well, you do have a tendency to get things all confused in that brilliant mind of yours."

"Oh, really? And how is that?"

Chris faced him, nose to nose. "I've always looked up to you, Jeremy. Always believed you had so much confidence, the way you ran Hamilton Media. I envied that, wished I could have that same kind of passion."

"But?"

"But lately, I've seen the other side of you. You ran away when the going got tough. Just left all of us in the middle of a crisis. I never thought I'd see the day—"

Anger edged down Jeremy's spine as he interrupted. "I never thought I'd see the day that I wouldn't be a Hamilton, little brother. You'll just have to forgive me for getting a bit out of sorts over this."

"I do forgive you," Chris replied, his tone soft and low. "We all do, and we certainly understand how you must feel. But I also think it's about time you forgive yourself, for whatever wrong you think you've done."

"Not being a Hamilton—that's my wrong," Jeremy said.

"But it's not your fault, and you're still a Hamilton, as far as we're all concerned."

Jeremy smiled again. "So get over myself?"

"Something like that," Chris replied. Then he

slapped Jeremy on the back. "I'm going to find Felicity. She's in a better mood than you."

Jeremy watched as Chris walked away, then turned to find Wallace staring at him. His mother glanced from her husband's face to Jeremy, a gentle plea in her eyes.

Jeremy's heart seemed to be pumping too hard against his chest. He wouldn't make a scene here at his sister's wedding. But he had to at least make an effort. Searching, he found Gabi in the crowd. Her expression of daring and challenge gave him the courage to move forward.

Motioning for her, he waited as she crossed the room. Then he took her by the hand. "I want you to meet my father," he said.

Gabi let out a relieved breath. She had wondered all night if Jeremy would speak with Wallace. "All right." Her gaze never wavered. She wanted so much to give Jeremy the encouragement he needed to get through this awkward moment.

Jeremy held her hand tightly in his as they moved across the long room. When they reached the table where Nora sat with Wallace, Jeremy inclined his head. "Hello, Mom. You remember Gabi, right?"

Nora stood up, beaming. "Of course I do." Taking Gabi's hand, she smiled at her. "It's so good to see you again." Then she turned to Wallace. "This is Gabi Valencia, dear. She's a friend of Jeremy's."

Ever the gentleman, Wallace pushed himself up out of his chair, the effort causing him to tremble.

"Hello," he said, his gaze moving from Gabi to Jeremy.

Gabi watched as he gave Jeremy a strained smile, but neither man said anything.

"It's good to see you out of the hospital, Mr. Hamilton," Gabi said, concerned that he might give out and slump over. "Please, sit back down."

But Wallace remained standing, his discomfort evident as he turned to face Jeremy. "Hello, son."

Gabi watched as Jeremy's expression turned to stone. His father had called him son, but Jeremy looked as unyielding as the mountains beyond the Cumberland River. "Hello, sir."

"Will you sit with us for a while?" Nora asked.

Gabi looked to Jeremy. "That would be nice."

Jeremy pulled out a chair for her, then sank down beside his mother. The tension surrounding them seemed to cut them off from the rest of the laughing, happy crowd.

"It was a beautiful ceremony," Gabi said to break the silence.

"Yes, very lovely," Nora replied, her nervous gaze moving back and forth between the two men sitting at opposite ends of the table. "The whole family helped to put it all together. Everyone has been so good during my husband's illness—"

"You're blessed with a loving family," Gabi said. She saw Jeremy's little flinch and knew she'd struck an unintentional blow.

"Yes, we certainly are," Nora replied. "I'm so

thankful that each of our children has found some happiness. That is the best medicine."

Wallace looked over at Jeremy, but he didn't say a word. His expression said everything. Gabi could see the pain and the defeat there in his vivid eyes. And she could also see the hope and the need for redemption. She felt that same hope inside her own confused soul.

Jeremy tore his gaze away from his parents. "Would you like some more punch?" he asked Gabi.

She could see that he really wanted to leave this table. She could also see that the whole crowd had noticed Jeremy sitting with his parents. It was as if the entire gathering had slowed and stopped, everyone holding their collective breaths to see what would happen next.

"I'm fine," she managed to say, even though her throat was as dry as the oak leaves scattered down in the park.

Finally, Wallace placed a hand down on the table. "Jeremy, could I have a word with you, in private?"

Jeremy lifted his head to stare across the table at his father. "I'm not so sure—"

"I really need to tell you something," Wallace said, his voice hoarse and husky.

Gabi saw the confusion clouding Jeremy's face, saw the fight within his soul. She moved to get up, but Jeremy's hand on her arm held her back, though his eyes were on his father. His next words were gentle and whispered. "Not now, Father. I'm glad you're better, but I'm not ready to have this discussion. Not here at Melissa's wedding."

"Then when?" Wallace asked, his voice rising.

People turned to stare.

"I don't know," Jeremy said, taking Gabi by the hand to pull her away. "I don't know."

She whirled around, hoping to apologize to Nora.

Nora's smile was etched with tension. "It was good to see you again, Gabi."

Gabi nodded, waved her free hand. "I hope you continue to improve, Mr. Hamilton."

But Wallace wasn't listening. He was watching as his oldest son moved to make a quick escape from the table.

Jeremy tugged Gabi through the stunned crowd, not stopping even as Gabi grabbed their coats and her purse, until they were outside in the crisp December twilight.

Only then did he let her go, his breath coming in great huffs, as if he couldn't get enough of the clean, cold air.

Gabi stood watching him, her heart hurting both for his parents and for Jeremy. She couldn't imagine the depth of his despair or the range of his humiliation. This man, this gentle, brilliant, hardworking, good man, had had his whole world ripped out from under him.

She didn't know how he'd ever overcome that. But she prayed that somehow he would.

And she made a promise to God that she would help Jeremy. Because she knew how it felt to think there was no hope left. She had to show him that there *was* hope, and that together they could find redemption. That meant she had to open up to him and be honest.

Reaching out a hand to him, she said, "Jeremy, I know how it feels to blame yourself for things you can't control. You have to understand that what's happened isn't your fault."

He turned to stare at her as if he couldn't believe her. "But it *is* my fault. I'm not a Hamilton. My whole life has been a sham."

Anger coursed through Gabi, making her hold his arm tightly, her fingers pressing into the sleeve of his coat. "No, it hasn't. You've worked hard, carried the weight of your family. You did everything right—"

"And look where that got me."

She bobbed her head, her breath coming too quickly, making it hard to speak. "I did everything right, too. Or so I thought. But sometimes, that doesn't matter. Sometimes life just…goes wrong. We can't let that paralyze us. You have to get over this, or you won't ever be happy again."

"Even with you, you mean?"

"Yes, even with me, if that's what you think you want."

He turned to tug her close, his eyes moving over her face. "Right now, you're the only thing I want."

Gabi pulled away. "But I'm not ready to bear that burden."

"I'm a burden to you?"

"You're a burden I could willingly carry, but that would be wrong. You need to get through this yourself. You can't depend on me—you're just using me to hide your pain."

"That's not true. I want to be with you."

She turned to gaze up at him. "I believe that. I do. But I want you to feel the same way once this crisis is over."

"So you think I won't need you forever?"

"I'm saying you need to think things through very carefully and not substitute me for your family." She looked out over the trees and mountains. "I can see how much you long to just turn back time, but that can't happen. The only thing you can do now is look to the future, look forward to beginning your life all over again. You can learn from this."

"Oh, I'm learning, all right," he said, his voice cold and a monotone. He pushed away, his shoulders slumped, his hands fisted.

"Don't do that," Gabi said, pulling him back around to face her. "Not with me. I'm here and I'm willing to stand by you, but…I let one man down before. I don't want to let you down in the same way."

Jeremy pivoted then, his expression changing from cold and harsh to soft and yielding. "Your husband?"

She could only nod, unable to speak. But her whole body trembled with a crippling guilt. "Can you just give me some time, Jeremy?"

He put his hands on her arms, held her there. "I think I can do that. I'm sorry for the way I've been acting."

"I understand."

"You're right," he said, guiding her toward the car. "I still have a lot to work through. But you've helped me so much. Painting that wall helped me. And I did at least speak to my father tonight."

"You're going to be okay."

He opened the car door. "Thanks for being honest with me."

Gabi sat looking at the church steeple. It shimmered with a glow from the streetlights. She hadn't been completely honest, because much of what she'd just criticized him about could easily apply to her. She was frozen in the past, too. How could she fuss at Jeremy when she'd been acting the very same way?

When he got in beside her, he said, "One day, I want to hear all the details about what really happened between you and your husband."

"One day," she said. He didn't question her. He just grabbed her hand and held it as they sat in the dark.

Chapter Twelve

"Margie, please screen all my calls."

Jeremy hung up the phone, determined to get some work done this morning. He hadn't slept very well, and this Monday was already proving to be hectic and full of problems. An office administrator in classifieds had given her two weeks notice, a features reporter was out sick, and everyone was rushing around with last-minute holiday jitters. If he had one more interruption, he was going to go home, put on his jogging clothes and run through Sugar Tree Park until he couldn't breathe.

But you've been running all fall, remember? Now, he felt so tired, as if he had indeed been running a long, hard race with no end in sight. Gabi's tough words kept echoing through his head. And his father's expectant face kept moving through both his dreams and his sleeplessness.

It was one week until Christmas, but Jeremy couldn't find much to celebrate. Except for Gabi. While his brothers and sisters constantly coaxed him to make amends with their father, Gabi had given it to him straight up. He couldn't move forward because he was frozen in the past. Even though she'd told him the truth, she'd also given him her support and her understanding. And made him see that he'd never be whole again until he made some changes.

Remembering how much he'd enjoyed taking her to Melissa's wedding, he also remembered how he'd dragged her out of the crowded reception hall, every eye in the room following them after his brief confrontation with his father.

His father. Would he ever get used to calling Wallace that again?

"I didn't handle that too well, did I?" he'd asked Gabi after rushing her to the car last night. They'd sat there a while, silent, holding hands until he'd finally let out a breath and asked her that question.

"You did speak to him. It's a start."

Her soft-spoken reply no longer held any censure.

"I just can't bring myself to sit down and talk to the man. I know he wants us to be close again, but it's hard."

Gabi had encouraged him to keep trying. "He's getting better now, Jeremy. He almost died, but he has a chance to make up for what he's done to you. That has to be part of the healing."

Jeremy thought about her words now, wondering if he could make a difference in his father's recovery simply by giving in and acknowledging Wallace. He'd have to try, for his mother's sake, and maybe for his own sanity. Gabi had been talking about him doing some healing of his own, too.

He worked on a stack of papers, signing off on budget reports and marketing promotions, then did some work on his computer for the next hour, pleasant memories of kissing Gabi good night making him stop and smile as he stared out at the mountain peaks in the distance.

Margie burst in just as the clock ticked toward noon, causing Jeremy to glance up from the papers he had yet to read. "Uh, Jeremy, your dad just called. He wants you to call him back."

Surprised that Wallace had made the effort, Jeremy held back from picking up the phone immediately to return the call. "Thanks, Margie. Anything else?"

His phone shrilled out three concise rings even as he asked the question. Margie quickly picked it up, her lips lifting into an indulgent smile as she glanced over at Jeremy. "Let me see if he's available," she said.

Jeremy shook his head, but Margie held up a hand. "Yes, I understand. Roni—Veronica. Got it. And Talia. You both need to talk to Mr. Hamilton?"

Jeremy waved his hand. "I'll take that call."

Margie grinned, then handed him the receiver. "Sounds urgent."

"Roni?" Jeremy asked, hoping nothing was wrong at the Valencia house. "Are you okay, sweetheart?"

Roni giggled. "We're fine, Mr. Jeremy. Our grandmother said we could call you."

"Shouldn't you be in school?" Jeremy asked, enjoying the giggles from the other end of the phone.

"We're out for the holidays," Roni explained in an overly patient tone. "But we need your help."

Confused, but pleased that the formidable little Roni had reached out to him, Jeremy said, "Okay. What's the problem?"

Talia's cute voice echoed over the line before her sister could speak. "We want to buy Mama a nice present. Will you take us shopping?"

Shopping for Gabi. Jeremy hadn't even thought about Christmas presents. "Of course, but how does your grandmother feel about this?"

"She said we'd have to clear it with Mama, but we can't tell Mama who we're shopping for—you know, since it's her. We begged *Abuela* to let us call you."

"I understand," Jeremy replied. "But why me?"

Roni took over again. "Because we told our grandmother you like Mama and you'll help us pick her out something special. *Abuela* already has all her gifts for Mama."

"I see," Jeremy said, grinning. Maybe Gabi's mom was in on this matchmaking scheme right along with Dawn. "Well, I think I can arrange some time later this afternoon. But you have to make sure your mother gives you her permission." He glanced at the clock. "I'll call her at work just to clear it, okay?"

"Okay," Roni replied. "Can you pick us up at our *abuela's* house?"

"Sure." Jeremy took down the address. The house wasn't far from Gabi's. He agreed to pick them up around four that afternoon, if Gabi gave her approval.

He looked up at Margie's grinning face. "Thanks, Margie. I have another call to make."

"Sure thing," Margie said, backing out of the room.

Jeremy dialed Gabi's work number. She answered on the second ring. "Hi, it's me," he said.

"Hi." She sounded hesitant. "How are you?"

"I'm doing just fine. Busy."

"Me, too."

He didn't like the stilted tone in her voice. Did she think he was angry with her? "I need to ask you something," he said, trying to sound light.

He heard her sigh. "Okay. Go ahead."

He got right to the point. "Your girls want me to take them shopping."

That got her attention. "Why? What are you talking about?" He could hear the anxiety in her voice.

"It's a big secret. We're going to shop for someone very special, so I can't tell you any more than that."

"I see." He heard her chuckle then. "Are you sure you're ready to go shopping with two little girls?"

"I guess I'll find out."

"Jeremy, you don't have to do this."

"Yes, I do. I insist. I just wanted to clear it with you."

She was silent a minute, then said, "I guess it's okay. Just don't let them drag you all over the place."

"We'll be fine. And we'll bring dinner home for you."

"That's not—" She stopped, sighed. "My Sunday

school Christmas party is tonight. You could bring them to meet me there." She named the restaurant and time. "And you can stay a while, if you'd like."

"Great. See you later."

After hanging up, Jeremy looked at the work piled on his desk, then tackled it with new energy. He had to get this done so he could help the girls pick out something nice for their mother. And he'd find Gabi a special gift from him, too. Whistling along with the jazzy holiday tune playing over the radio, Jeremy finally got into the Christmas spirit.

"That one sure is pretty."

Roni looked longingly at the gold necklace with the dainty diamonds set in a sparkling row of three, one on top of the other.

"It has three diamonds," Talia said, grinning up at Jeremy. "One for Mommy and one for each of us."

"So it does," Jeremy said, giving the clerk behind the jewelry counter at Engel's a heads-up. "Could we have a closer look at that one?"

The clerk, a young blond woman, nodded her approval. "That's a good choice, Mr. Hamilton."

Surprised that she knew him, Jeremy looked at the price of the necklace. It was expensive. Careful to hide that fact from the girls, he made a big deal of surveying the necklace. "What do you think, Roni?"

Roni looked from the glistening necklace to him. "I think we didn't bring enough money."

The disappointment in her eyes made Jeremy's heart do funny things. He looked at the clerk, hoping she'd heed his meaning. "Oh, I think you brought just enough money. How much do you have?"

"Together, about twenty-two dollars," Talia said. "It's our allowance and some *Abuela* gave us."

"Just right," Jeremy replied, nodding to the clerk. "Could you wrap this up extra special for the girls?" Then he leaned close, his charge card in one hand. "This should cover the wrapping paper and…anything else needed."

"Of course, Mr. Hamilton," the girl whose name tag read Lyn, said, bobbing her head. "I'll take care of this right away."

Jeremy spotted the matching earrings. "Lyn, add these to our purchases, too, will you?"

Lyn took the earrings out of the case.

"Are we buying those, too?" Talia asked, glancing up at Jeremy with big eyes.

"Those are from me, but not a word to your mother."

Both girls giggled behind their hands.

"She's gonna flip," Talia said.

"Thank you," Roni added shyly. "That was nice of you."

Jeremy beamed a smile at her. "I wanted to give your mother something, too, so now we have that all taken care of. What next?"

"Can I go talk to Santa?" Talia asked. "I need to ask him something really bad."

Jeremy looked at Roni. "I guess we could do that

while Lyn is finishing with your mother's gifts. Is that okay with you, Roni?"

Roni shook her head, one hand on her hip. "I don't believe in Santa, but Talia thinks she has to talk to him." She shrugged, her indifference making her look mature beyond her years. "I guess she can go."

Jeremy told Lyn they'd be back for the packages in a few minutes, then took the girls to the toy department. Santa had set up shop right there in the store.

Talia rushed up to the big red velvet chair, waving to the bearded man who sat ready to listen to Christmas requests. "Hello, Santa."

"Well, hello there, little lady," the jolly Santa replied. "What can I do for you today?"

Jeremy stood back with Roni, noting how she tried to look bored. "Don't you want to talk to Santa?"

She looked at her glitter-covered nails. "No, sir."

"But isn't there something you want for Christmas?"

Roni finally looked up at him. "Not really. I'll get clothes and maybe some CDs, but Santa can't bring me what I really want."

Jeremy went down on one knee so he could look her in the eye. "And what's that, honey?"

Roni shrugged again, her big eyes pinning Jeremy with a direct look. "Talia wants to ask Santa for a new daddy. I told her that's dumb. Why should we get a new daddy?" Her next words caused

Jeremy to flinch. "I want my daddy back. And even Santa can't make that happen."

Jeremy didn't know how to answer that. But he certainly knew how Roni felt. "It's tough to lose someone you love," he said. "Have you talked to your mother about this?"

"She knows," Roni replied, tapping a sneakered foot. "I hear her sometimes, at night. She cries. So I try not to worry her too much." Then she looked up at him. "That's why I'm trying to like you, too."

Roni's gentle admission floored Jeremy. He looked right into her eyes. "Honey, I'd love to be your friend, but I know I can never replace your daddy." He couldn't tell her that he knew exactly how she felt, that he'd never known his own biological father. But he could certainly try to make Roni understand. "I don't want you or your mother ever to fight or disagree over me. I wouldn't do that to you."

Roni shrugged, her tiny shoulders looking fragile. "It's just hard...sometimes. I don't like to see Mama crying, but I don't like to see her with you either. Are you mad at me for telling you that?"

Jeremy touched the child's arm. "Of course I'm not mad. I'm glad you told me. It just means you love your mother and that you still remember your father. I think that is very admirable."

Roni's soft smile tugged at his heart. "Does that mean we're okay—you and me?"

"We sure are, even if you're not so sure about

having me around. And I don't want to make either you or your mother cry, okay?"

"Okay."

Jeremy closed his eyes to that image. He never wanted to see Gabi crying. He wanted to make her happy again. But how could he do that when he still had the same sort of grief deep inside himself? And he couldn't explain to Roni that he, too, had lost a father, in more ways than one.

Talia came running up to them. "I told Santa what I wanted."

"And what did he say?" her sister asked, her question challenging.

Talia waved to Santa. "He said he would send up a special prayer for me."

"But he didn't promise you a new daddy, did he?"

"Not really," Talia said. "But he's Santa. He can make anything happen."

"No, he can't," Roni retorted. Then she tugged on Jeremy's coat. "Tell her, Mr. Jeremy. Tell her that Santa isn't real and he can't bring her a daddy."

Jeremy felt Talia's little hand on his. "I don't care what Roni thinks. I believe in Santa. And I believe that one day, he'll bring me a nice person to love Mommy and us."

"Whatever," Roni said, breaking away with yet another shrug. But she gave Jeremy a hopeful look, in spite of her attempts to be nonchalant.

Talia still held tightly to Jeremy's hand. "Do you believe in Santa?" she asked.

Jeremy felt the prick of tears in his eyes. "I want

to, honey. I sure want to." Then he leaned down to swoop her up into his arms. "Maybe your sister just doesn't want you to get your hopes up. Bringing toys is very different, compared to what you're asking Santa for."

"I know," Talia replied, her tone pragmatic. "That's why I asked for a baby doll, too."

That made Jeremy laugh in spite of the rip inside his heart. "Now I know for a fact that Santa can deliver on that request."

After having hot chocolate at Betty's, Jeremy took the girls to meet Gabi at her class Christmas party at a large restaurant out on the river. The group had gathered in a private room at the back of the seafood restaurant. When Jeremy entered with the girls, everyone smiled and waved.

Dawn hugged the girls close, while Gabi smiled at Jeremy. "Thanks for bringing them. And for taking them shopping."

"No problem," he said, glad to see her smiling face.

She was dressed in black pants and a red sweater woven with glittery gold threads. Her hair was down and curling around her face. She looked relaxed and happy. He remembered Roni's earlier words, about Gabi crying at night. He never wanted to cause her any pain.

"So what's the big secret about this shopping trip?" she asked, grinning down at the girls.

"It's still a secret," Talia replied, hiding her

giggles behind her hand. "You have to wait until Christmas."

"Oh, I see." She leaned close to Jeremy. "So my girls got you involved in this, huh?"

"It was fun. I enjoyed being with them."

"And we talked to Santa," Talia said, hopping with excitement.

"You did. I didn't," Roni said, stomping away to talk to some of her friends.

"She's at that age," Gabi said to Jeremy. "She's having a hard time this year."

Jeremy didn't tell Gabi what Roni and he had talked about. Instead, he said, "I think she wishes with all her heart for Santa to be real."

"Don't we all?"

He smiled at that, then took her hand in his. "I sure feel as if he's brought me a nice present."

She blushed and looked down. "This has been an interesting Christmas."

"And it's not over yet."

"That's right. We have the Christmas play tomorrow night. You *are* coming, right?"

"I wouldn't miss it," he told her.

Her dark eyes held his. "Jeremy, about last night—"

"I had a wonderful time."

"I mean, I'm sorry I was so harsh with you, after we talked to your father."

"Hey, I needed to hear that."

"So you're not mad at me?"

Her words and tone reminded him of Roni asking him the very same question.

"No. I appreciate what you said."

"And you'll…give us some time?"

"Of course. And in the meantime, I intend to win you over—after I change my ways, of course."

"I don't want you to change. I just want you to be very clear about your feelings."

"Oh, I'm clear on that," he said, his gaze moving over her face. "I just need to make sure you understand things. I'm not using you. But I'm willing to wait. And you're right. I need to move on and…celebrate all that's good in my life."

She lifted her head, her smile reinforcing that statement. "We both need to do that."

They turned to all the friends gathered together to celebrate the holidays. Jeremy raised his punch glass to his brother Chris. Felicity was here, along with Ethan and Heather, and Bryan and Amy. Tim and Dawn had just left to visit Wallace. Jeremy wondered if he shouldn't do the same. And he probably should start attending this class at church, since most of his siblings and the woman he was attracted to were members.

Spending the afternoon with Talia and Roni had taught him a valuable lesson: being a parent wasn't easy. Children were so innocent, so vulnerable, but so very wise and all-seeing. He could now understand why his parents had tried to protect him for so long. Their love for him had forced them to withhold the truth.

Later, as he stood at Gabi's door with her in his arms, he thought again about his father. "I enjoyed tonight," he told her. "And I really enjoyed shopping with the girls."

"Thanks again," she said, looking up at him, her eyes as dark and rich as the earth surrounding the river. "They don't get to indulge themselves very much."

"I'd spoil them rotten," he said, meaning it.

"You can't do that," she quickly replied.

"I'd spoil you, too, if you'd let me."

"I know," she said, shaking her head. "That's why I have to resist you."

"So I *am* tempting?"

She smiled, touched a hand to his face. "Too tempting."

Talia stuck her head out the door. "Mommy, I'm ready for bed. Come tuck me in." Then she reached a hand to Jeremy. "You, too, Mr. Jeremy."

Jeremy knew right then that he was a goner. Not only did he love Gabi, but he loved her daughters, too. Looking to Gabi for guidance, he asked, "May I?"

Gabi seemed hesitant, but she finally nodded. "If that's what Talia wants."

"I do, I do," Talia said, doing her famous foot-hopping dance. Then she held her arms wide for Jeremy.

He took her up, holding the little girl close as they entered the house. Talia's unconditional trust and acceptance made him feel both humble and blessed.

Watching Gabi read a short Bible story to Talia only added to the emotional overload he'd been feeling lately. He kissed the little girl good night, then told her stoic sister Roni he'd see her soon.

Then he held Gabi close, unable to say what was in his heart.

But when he left the Valencia house about an hour later, he headed straight home to the Hamilton estate. It was past bedtime, but Jeremy let himself in the back door and walked quietly and steadily to the small study on the first floor where his father's hospital bed had been placed. The night nurse they'd hired to sit with Wallace told Jeremy his mother was asleep upstairs. Jeremy asked the whispering nurse to take a break. Then he was alone with Wallace.

Glad for that, Jeremy stood just inside the door, in the dark, watching the rise and fall of his father's chest. He stood, his heart beating against the wool of his jacket, his mind reeling with wave after wave of emotion—pain, anger, rejection, regret, fear and, finally, a need so great he almost bent over with it.

"I understand so much now, Father," he said, his words a soft whisper. "I know you didn't mean to hurt me. I know you love me." He wiped at the hot tears forming in his eyes. "I so wanted to be like you. I wanted to be your son. I wanted you to be proud of me."

He waited, listening to the silence, listening to Wallace's steady breathing. "Can you forgive me, Daddy? Can you forgive me for turning away?"

Jeremy stopped, took in a breath. He realized he

wasn't just talking to his living father, here in this room. He was also asking God to forgive him, too. He'd turned away from both, his rage and his need too great to comprehend. Now he understood the only way to ease that rage and pain was to forgive and to turn back to God. He had to let go of the past so he could have a new and better future. And the first step would be to reconcile with the man in this bed.

He moved toward the bed, touched a hand to his father's aged fingers. "I'm here, Daddy. I'm here. I just want you to know that." He held Wallace's hand in his for a long time, his prayers centered on healing for both of them.

"I'm so sorry, Daddy."

Then he turned and left the room.

Wallace woke with a start. "Jeremy?"

He glanced around, the light from the bathroom illuminating the empty room. He'd heard Jeremy's voice. He knew it. He'd heard his son's words of encouragement, words of hope and forgiveness. "Jeremy?" he called out again.

There was no answer.

Maybe he'd been dreaming, but for the first time in many months, Wallace smiled and felt a deep peace inside his soul. And then he slept the night through.

Chapter Thirteen

"You can't back out on me now, darlin'."

Ellen Manning stared over at the man sitting in her car on the outskirts of Hickory Mills. "I can and I will, Curtis. I'm tired of your promises. Tired of doing your dirty work for you."

Curtis let out a long-suffering sigh. "You truly try my patience, you know that?"

Ellen had had enough of his sweet talk and his empty promises. "Patience? I don't have any of that left myself. For months now, you've been promising me this whole new life in Nashville with you. But you keep hanging around, snooping into the Hamiltons' business. And for what? Revenge? You think they did you wrong?"

"They *did* do me wrong," Curtis said, his words sliding out between clenched teeth. Ellen recognized all the signs of his rage, but she wasn't as in awe of him as she'd been months ago. In spite of being scared, now she just felt sorry for him. Still, she had to be careful.

She'd thought about just going to Jeremy Hamilton and telling him the truth. But then, she didn't want to have to deal with that, either. Curtis would be furious and might come after her. She had to wonder why none of the Hamiltons had put two and two together and figured this out, but Curtis had assured her he'd covered his tracks. He'd left Hamilton Media with a smile on his face, and a promise to Jeremy to stay in touch. That smile was now gone, and the only staying in touch he'd done was through back-alley meetings and using her as a spy.

"Look," she said, glancing around to make sure no one was watching them, "we've gotten all the goods on the Hamiltons. There's nothing left. And they're still going strong. Rumors roll right off them, Curtis. What more can we do?"

The gloomy gray afternoon only added to her misery. She felt dirty, sitting here with Curtis. Here it was, Christmas time, but Ellen felt anything but happy. Why did she always let men control her life?

"I told you—I have one more ace up my sleeve," Curtis retorted, his features harsh and angular. "I just need a little more time, honey." Then he leaned close, his words threatening. "And I need a little more information—from you."

Ellen hit the steering wheel. "I don't have anything else."

Curtis touched a hand to her gloved fingers. "Think real hard."

Ellen's heart started squirming. This man could be dangerous. At first, that had been part of his attraction. But now, it only frightened her. Deciding to give him anything to get him off her back, she said, "Oh, all right. The big Hamilton office Christmas party is Friday night. I heard some workers talking about it at Betty's this morning."

"At Hamilton Media?"

"Yes. That might be a good time to…finish things up."

"A perfect time," Curtis said, nodding. "I can get in and out without anyone being the wiser, since they'll all be downstairs celebrating their good fortune." He gave her a quick kiss. "You did good, girl."

"I'm done," Ellen said. "Do you hear me?"

"You might want to crash that party," Curtis said, his eyes gleaming. "You always were so great at distracting Jeremy Hamilton. Use your charms on him again, for me."

Ellen shook her head. "Jeremy never cared about me." She'd long ago gotten over that, but it still hurt. "He's got a new girlfriend."

Curtis laughed. "The *chica* from across the tracks? Please! That won't last long. Jeremy is just slumming it, since none of the society ladies will give him the time of day." He tugged at his topcoat. "I've checked her out. She doesn't have a clue about anything. But she sure has eyes for Hamilton. Probably wants his money to get her across the tracks and more upscale."

Shocked, Ellen leaned back against her seat. "You've spied on Gabriela Valencia?"

Curtis chuckled. "I've gone by the hospital a couple of times, to watch her at work. Just in case I could get something else on Hamilton, or just in case I needed a source at the hospital. But he's such a gentleman, as pure as snow. Their whole relationship is boring and downright pathetic. He goes by her house a lot, but he never stays too late. He's even taken her kids shopping. A regular family man."

"I wouldn't underestimate him," Ellen warned. "He's changed, Curtis. He's not as soft and forgiving as he was when you tried to swindle him."

Curtis grabbed her arm, making her wince. "I didn't swindle anybody. Hamilton owed me that money, and I aim to get the rest of what he owes me, too."

Ellen had never understood what spreading rumors could possibly gain, but then she'd been so caught up in Curtis's charm and her own failings, she would have done anything to help him get back at the Hamiltons. Now, she just wanted to be away from Curtis and away from Davis Landing. Maybe after Christmas, things would change.

"Why do you need more information? If the Hamiltons owe you something, why don't you just ask them for it?"

"Me, beg the Hamiltons?" He hit a hand on the dashboard. "I'm through begging. But I know how to get my hands on some of their money. I need records, darlin'. Records and receipts. Then I can take what I need and blow this sorry excuse for a town."

"Why can't we just leave now, together?" Ellen

asked, wishing she had the nerve to do just that—with or without Curtis.

Curtis turned harsh again, his expression full of irritation. "I told you, I need some sort of insurance, and I need cash. We won't get very far on my unemployment checks."

"I just don't like the idea of stealing, Curtis."

He leaned close, rubbed a hand over her cheek. "The Hamiltons don't mind stealing one bit, sugar. They took from me and they humiliated you, or have you forgotten?"

"I haven't forgotten anything."

"Good, then just keep watch and let me do what I need to do."

"I'd better get back," she said, looking out over the rain-drenched woods.

"Yeah, go on back to the *Observer* and work hard," Curtis said, his mocking tone making Ellen wince again. "Meantime, I'll figure out how to get into Hamilton's office and find those files I need."

"You'd better be careful."

He grinned, then opened the door. "Like I said, darlin', in and out. Then this will finally be over."

"I hated to see it end," Jeremy whispered to Gabi as he led her out of the church later that night. "The play was great. Especially that scenery."

"Yes, the scenery was obviously painted by a master," Gabi said, her smile reflecting the happiness in her heart. "But my girls are stars. Talia was a perfect little angel and Roni did a great job of being Mary, don't you think?"

"I do, and I've got about thirty pictures to prove it," Jeremy said, patting the digital camera in his pocket. "I'll get these to you right away."

"Thanks," Gabi replied. "I guess I'd better gather the girls and get them home. It'll take all night to settle them down."

"I could come, too," Jeremy offered. "We could order a pizza."

Gabi considered that offer, wondering when exactly it had become so easy to spend time with Jeremy. Maybe from the first moment they'd met? "Pizza sounds good. They had crackers and cheese before the play, but I'm sure they're probably starving now that it's over."

"Then it's a date?"

"Yes," she said, thinking she'd been with Jeremy just about every night for the last week or so. It would be so hard, after the holidays, to taper off from seeing him. But she wondered if it wouldn't happen that way. He'd go back to his life, once he'd settled back down at Hamilton Media. Everyone said his father would be well soon, and then what?

"Are you sure?" he asked, as if sensing her hesitancy. "I know you wanted to take things slow, but—"

"I'm sure," she replied, pushing away thoughts of what might happen next. "I'm getting used to having you around."

"In spite of my shortcomings?"

"Maybe because of your shortcomings," she teased. "I wouldn't want you to be perfect."

He leaned close. "Well, I think you're perfect."

"I'm not," she said, her tone insistent. "Honestly, Jeremy, I don't want you thinking that."

"Hey, it was a joke," he said, confusion clouding his features. "But I have to say, so far, I can't find one thing to complain about."

Gabi wanted to bask in the glow of his compliments, but she still wasn't so sure of herself. She'd asked God to guide her in her feelings toward Jeremy, and somehow, they'd settled into an easy routine of talking on the phone and sharing social events together. And now, pizza with the girls. Things were moving right along, in spite of her resolve to keep things casual. It was hard to say no to Jeremy.

"What's wrong then?" Jeremy asked, bringing her out of her silence.

"Nothing," she admitted. "I like you, too. I can't find much to complain about either, even though I like to tease you."

That made him grin. "I'm growing on you, right?"

"Right." She laughed as the girls ran up to them. Laughed and felt a tug deep inside her heart as Jeremy took Talia into his arms as if she belonged right there.

"My stars," he said, holding on to Talia while he put a hand on Roni's back. "Pizza? I'm buying."

Talia squealed, but Roni suddenly looked mutinous. "We want to go to *Abuela's*. She said we could, after the play. She said she made a special cake for us."

"Is she expecting us?" Gabi asked, her gaze touching on Jeremy's face. She glanced around for her family, then saw her mother coming toward them.

"Probably," Roni said, glancing up at Jeremy. "But I don't think she knew about *him* coming, too."

Talia squealed again. "You can meet our family," she said to Jeremy. "They've all been asking about you."

"Have they?" Jeremy looked as if he'd been caught in a bear trap.

Then Marisol Marquez came up. "Hi," she said to Gabi, giving her a kiss on the cheek. "So are you coming over for cake?"

Gabi looked up at Jeremy. He didn't seem so sure. "We were just talking about that, Mama. We were going for pizza, but the girls want to see this special cake you made. And eat it, too."

"I'll order pizza, too, then," Marisol said, her tone hopeful, her smile warm as she gave Jeremy a questioning look. "You are welcome to come, too, Jeremy. I made my famous fudge cake—very choc-olaty."

Jeremy's manners kicked in. He smiled at Gabi's mother. "I do have a weakness for chocolate. Thanks for including me." Then he turned to Gabi. "Is that what you'd rather do?"

"We could go by there, if that's okay with you," Gabi said, hoping she could salvage both his pride and her eldest daughter's defenses. "We don't have to stay long."

"Is that all right with you, Roni?" Jeremy asked, his gaze gentle and questioning.

"What do you think, honey?" Gabi asked, noting Roni's stiff, unyielding body language. She stood with her arms crossed, a frown marring her youthful face. How could the girl be so happy with Jeremy one day, then pouting about him the next? She leaned close. "Remember, he did take you shopping. We owe him a piece of Grandmama's cake, at least."

"Sure," Roni said, tugging at her hair as she changed from challenging to contrite. "I didn't mean to sound selfish or mean, Mr. Jeremy."

Jeremy gently put Talia down, then bent to place a hand on Roni's arm. "I understand, Roni. You know, I have five brothers and sisters, but sometimes I like having my parents all to myself. If you'd rather just be with your family, without me there, I'll go on home."

Roni's big eyes turned soft as she gave him a steady gaze. "No, I want you to come. You'll love our *Abuelo*—he's really funny. And my uncles. And Aunt Yolanda. She's been wanting to meet you." She shrugged, tossing off her doubts and her disdain. "I guess I was just stressed about this play."

"Stressed?" Gabi smiled, then shook her head. "She never ceases to surprise me."

Jeremy grinned, pushed a hand through Roni's cascading curls, said, "Let's go then."

Gabi figured he was just being polite. "I'm sorry."

"It's okay," he said, his voice low as they walked to the car. "I'm being tested—by a very determined ten-year-old. Talk about *stressed*."

"She's just trying to protect herself," Gabi said.

"And her mother, too," Jeremy added.

"Are you sure you're up to meeting my entire family?"

"No, but I have to show courage. I can't let Roni see my fear."

Gabi laughed at that. "Oh, you'll need courage, that's for sure."

His expression was wry. "I can't wait."

They reached the car and after getting the girls inside, he turned to her. "But after the office party at Hamilton Media on Friday, I'm taking you out on a real date. Just the two of us. Alone. No pizza, no kids, no animals, no family, no well-meaning friends, no paintbrushes or cookie cutters. Just you and me, sitting down, with candlelight and good food and no interruptions. Okay?"

"Okay," she replied, a glow of joy filling her soul. She told herself she shouldn't be so excited, but her heart refused to heed that warning.

Two hours later, she grinned as Jeremy did an exaggerated slice with his hand across his throat, indicating he'd had enough. "Are you crying uncle?" she asked as she took his empty paper plate.

"Yes," he said through a groan. "Your parents are very nice, but your sister and those brothers—

I guess we should have told them I do know some Spanish."

"Why, what did they say?"

He shrugged, finished off his soda. "Oh, things like 'Mr. Big Britches,' 'Moneyman Hamilton,' and my favorite, 'not good enough for my sister.'"

"You interpreted all of that?"

"I got the gist of it, yes."

Gabi turned to where Yolanda sat with her husband, Pete, at the dining table in the kitchen. Pete sent Jeremy a sympathetic smile, but Yolanda stared openly at him, her dark brows lifted.

"You just need to ignore them," Gabi said, loud enough for her siblings to hear. "They should learn to mind their own business." She rapidly fired off her own comments in Spanish, shouting over toward the group.

Her brothers started laughing, and even Yolanda changed her glare into a grin. "Gabriela seems to be mad at us, *si?*"

Gabi nodded her head. "*Si!*"

Gabi's mother came over to the sink. "They have always been this way," she told Jeremy. "They love to tease their sisters about the men they bring home. Pete learned to endure it, but Yolanda seems to have forgotten the tears she cried in his defense when they were dating."

"I understand," Jeremy said. He shifted his gaze to Gabi, a steely determination clear in his eyes. "But they need to understand something, too, Mrs.

Marquez." He took Gabi's hand in his. "I don't scare that easily."

Gabi's heart seemed to melt right there. This man was strong and sure, in spite of all the setbacks he'd had lately. And she had to admit, since their talk after Melissa's wedding, Jeremy had seemed more sure and steady, his mood more lighthearted and positive. Maybe she could take a chance with him.

Marisol gave him an appreciative look. "I'll keep that in mind."

"I think you won her over," Gabi said, motioning for the girls as her mother walked away. "C'mon, we need to get home."

"I intend to win each of them over," Jeremy replied. "But mainly, I want to win you over."

Gabi saw the hope in his eyes. He would win them over, she knew. And he wouldn't do it with fancy gifts or by flashing his money around. He'd win her family over in the same way he'd *already* won her over. With his smile, with his convictions, with his steady faith and with his endearing, solid qualities. He'd painted a biblical scene on a wall for her. He'd taken her children shopping for her. He'd come here tonight, and he'd held his own with her overbearing sister and her overly macho brothers. For her.

Gabi was in love with Jeremy. But she didn't know how she was going to tell him that. Especially since she'd insisted that neither one of them was ready for this.

Maybe she was the one hiding behind excuses

from the past. She'd been a widow for several years now. But she'd used her grief as a shield against living life again. All of her being had been poured into keeping her girls safe and happy.

But what about me? She wondered now. Maybe it was time for her to take her own advice and… move on with her life. And maybe that life would include Jeremy.

Chapter Fourteen

"Well, I can't wait to get the bill for this one," Jeremy said to Tim. They were in the downstairs lobby at Hamilton Media and the office Christmas party was in full swing. "Exactly how much did we spend on this lavish spread, brother?"

Tim lifted a hand toward the Christmas tree shining brightly in the far corner. "Hey, it was worth it. We've had a rocky year, but we managed to stay on top of things. In spite of all the scandals, our subscriber bases with both the paper and the magazine are strong and our employees seem content—they all got Christmas bonuses."

Jeremy touched a hand to Tim's forehead.

"What?" Tim asked, moving his head away.

"Just checking for fever," Jeremy teased. "Who are you, and what did you do with my Scrooge brother?"

Tim laughed, slapped Jeremy across the back. "I was never that bad, was I?"

Jeremy nodded. "You used to grumble with every

gathering. You always wanted to be alone, upstairs, working. You had no time for celebrations." He conjured up a frown. "Now I guess I get to play bad boss, since I'm more of an executive than ever before."

"You don't like your new job here?"

Jeremy wasn't ready to answer that with complete honesty. "I didn't say that. I'm just still a bit restless."

Tim's dark eyebrows shot up. "You're distracted. Just like the rest of us, you have a new purpose."

"You mean, besides living and breathing Hamilton Media?"

"Exactly."

Tim glanced across the room at Dawn. Jeremy watched his brother's face light up as he waved at his intended. Dawn did look pretty in her blue-and-white Christmas sweater and flowing wool skirt. She had changed his brother, that was for sure. Wishing Gabi would hurry up and get here, Jeremy wondered if he wasn't a changed man himself. He'd certainly been through the fire lately. Now he felt as if he might just make it to the other side. And Gabi had helped him with that. He wanted to tell Tim all about his idea for the new magazine, but decided he'd do that later when there weren't so many people around. Besides, he wanted to tell Gabi about it first, since she'd planted the idea in his head.

"I'm happy for you and Dawn," he told his brother. "And it's good to see you actually celebrating with everyone else."

"I have a lot to celebrate this year," Tim said. "Dad is on the mend, the business is solid, and you came home."

Jeremy raised his cup of cider. "Not to mention, you are head-over-heels in love."

"Yes, there is that," Tim said, inching toward Dawn. "Got to go."

"I understand," Jeremy said, glancing around. He'd been waiting for Gabi near the lobby doors, the Gargoyles hovering nearby, their eyes sharp, their chuckles contagious as they rushed about making sure everyone had enough food and drink. But Jeremy couldn't relax until Gabi got here. Last time they'd talked, she said she'd be here by six. It was six-fifteen. Maybe he should call her again.

Or maybe he should just cool his engines. He started walking toward his mother. Nora held reign in a wing chair beside Wallace, who sat in a wheelchair basking in all the praise from family and friends. They'd come in while Jeremy was still upstairs, and had been surrounded by well-wishers since. Thinking he should at least have the courtesy to speak to his father, Jeremy stopped when Dr. Luke Strickland stepped in front of him.

"Jeremy, how have you been?"

Jeremy shook the doctor's hand, but a wall of resentment kept him from responding with a smile. "I'm doing okay, Luke."

Luke didn't look convinced. "Just okay?"

"I'm fine," Jeremy said. "Why do you ask?"

Luke ran a hand through his thick dark hair. "Look, I know you're angry at me—for not revealing what I knew about your paternity as soon as I found out. But you have to understand—"

"I know," Jeremy said, his hand going up. "Doctor-patient confidentiality."

Luke nodded. "That and the fact that I already knew you weren't a good donor match. I wish I could have spared you all this trouble, Jeremy. I just wanted to say I'm sorry."

Jeremy took a calming breath. He couldn't keep blaming everyone else for what he now knew to be the truth. He wasn't Wallace Hamilton's biological son, but for all of his life, he had been the firstborn son. That hadn't changed. Things could only get back to normal if he let go of all his pain and just accepted that he'd had a good life, and he'd been protected from the truth for his own sake.

"I'm okay, Luke," he finally said. "I'm working through all this, one day at a time. I don't hold it against you. You were just doing your job." He held out a hand. "And I'd like to thank you for that."

Luke's expression changed into a slight smile as he shook Jeremy's hand and relaxed back on his heels. "I'm glad you feel that way. These past few months, with Wallace in the hospital, it just wasn't the same without you."

Jeremy nodded. "You don't have to remind me of that. I'm back for good now."

"Good," Luke said. Then he gave Jeremy a playful punch on the arm. "And from what I hear, you're doing okay in the dating department these days, too."

Jeremy couldn't hide his smile. "I am. If my date would just show up."

He saw Tim motioning for him. "Look, Luke, my brother's signaling me. That probably means the presses are down or something else dire has happened. Enjoy the party."

Luke shook his hand again. "I'm glad we talked."

"Me, too." Then Jeremy leaned close. "And I hear a certain nurse might be interested in sharing a glass of punch with you."

Luke looked surprised. "Really now?"

Jeremy pointed to Tammy Franklin. According to his mother, Wallace's favorite nurse only had eyes for Dr. Strickland. The brown-haired, blue-eyed nurse had been watching them intently. "Wouldn't hurt to ask."

Luke actually looked nervous, but he lifted a hand in greeting. Tammy smiled and waved back. "You might be on to something."

"No, buddy, *you* might be on to something." Jeremy watched as Luke headed over to where Tammy stood with some of the other nurses from the hospital who'd helped Wallace through his illness. Tammy seemed very glad to see him.

Proud of his own matchmaking skills, Jeremy put off talking to his father to go and see what Tim wanted instead.

"Y'all look very serious," he said as he entered

the intimate circle a few feet from where his parents sat. Most of his siblings were there, minus their various significant others who were mingling with the merry crowd. Only Chris and Melissa were missing. Chris was on duty and was expected later and Melissa was talking to Richard and some other people on the other side of the room.

Jeremy noticed his father watching them with keen eyes. He nodded at Wallace and was rewarded with a shaky salute from his father.

"What's up?" he said, looking at Amy.

"We were just discussing the rumor thing," Tim said. "Have you had any luck narrowing it down?"

Jeremy let out a sigh. "If you mean, do I know who's doing this, then no. I've talked to as many people around town as possible, including Betty Owens. She assures me she's not involved and I believe her, and I never questioned her about Justine."

Tim leaned forward. "You don't actually believe Justine could be a Hamilton, do you?"

Jeremy looked toward their father, then back. "I don't know what to believe anymore. We can never be sure. But I didn't push the issue with Betty. That's between her and our father, if it is true."

"I don't believe it," Tim said, his voice rising and frustration causing him to scowl. "Anyway, back to business. I just want all this scandal to be over."

"So do I," Jeremy replied. "And I have been working on it. But no one here at the office can shed any light, either. I checked back over all the employee records, too, to see if anyone left mad. It

all started after we found out about Dad's illness."
He stopped, a light bulb going on inside his head.
"Hey, wait a minute."

"What is it?" Heather asked, her eyes going wide.

"When did Ellen Manning leave Hamilton
Media?"

"Right after…right after you left town," Heather
said, realization dawning in her eyes. "You don't
think—"

Jeremy held up a hand, trying to connect the
pieces. "You know, through this whole thing, I've
had this nagging thought that the answer was right
in front of us."

"You think Ellen might be that answer?" Tim
asked, careful to keep his voice low.

Jeremy figured his father was probably straining
to hear their conversation, so he spoke in hushed
tones. "I left town this summer, right after Dad
got so sick. And Ellen quit at about the same time,
right?"

Heather's head came up. "Yes, right after I had to
fill in as the subject at one of her Makeover Maven
shoots. We had a great shoot and everything was
fine, though she disappeared in the middle of it,
then she didn't show up for work the next day."

"Ellen was ditzy, but she always struck me as
very professional. It's odd how she left," Jeremy
said.

"Very," Amy echoed. "I've never made the connection, but these rumors *did* start circulating

after Ellen quit. And she quit a day after you left, Jeremy."

"And why exactly did she quit?" Jeremy asked.

"We never got an answer," Heather admitted. "She just up and left after I got the makeover. She insisted I do it, but do you think she resented me for stepping in that day?"

"Could be," Tim replied. "The woman was great at her job, but neurotic when it came to dealing with anyone who threatened her. Maybe after she talked you into it, she felt as if she'd shot herself in the foot—since you were such a great subject and a Hamilton to boot."

Amy nodded. "Ellen was kind of paranoid. And she had this way of dating the wrong men, which only added to her insecurities. She worried about other women taking her conquests away." Then she snapped her fingers. "If I remember correctly, she'd been dating someone new back then. She wouldn't even talk about him, though, which isn't like Ellen. She loved to brag about her relationships. A couple of times, she did let some tidbits slip, things like how he'd taken her to a fancy restaurant in Nashville and bought her jewelry, but she was very mysterious and closed-mouth about her new fellow."

"Where is she now?" Jeremy asked.

"We've heard she's working at the *Observer*," Tim said. When Jeremy looked surprised, he added, "It's not what you think. She's not a top reporter. I think she's more of a stringer and she writes ad copy on the side. Why she'd take a job like that is beyond me. She can't be making the same money she made here, and she's not the center of attention there, either. This is more of a background job."

"Why didn't any of you mention this connection?" Jeremy asked, his gaze moving from one concerned face to the other.

"Probably because we had too much else to worry about," Amy admitted. "Ellen Manning wasn't on our priority list, especially after she quit without giving notice." She shrugged. "Her new job didn't seem that high-profile, so I guess we never thought about it. With everything else going on, it didn't seem that important. And besides, reporters and other press workers switch jobs all the time. That's how we got Felicity and Ethan."

"Okay," Jeremy said, nodding. "I think I need to check Ellen out. Even if she's not involved, she might be able to tell us if someone over at the *Observer* is deliberately supplying scandalous things about our family. No one else is willing to talk. Maybe Ellen will, if I corner her and hint at a libel suit."

Heather let out a gasp as she looked toward the front doors of the lobby. "Well, now's your chance, Jeremy. Ellen Manning just walked in the door."

Wallace Hamilton had heard enough of the hush-hush conversation in the corner to know he had to take care of a few details before he could start his life over again. Everyone had been tiptoeing around him lately, trying to keep any bad news away from him. But he still had his own sources, in spite of being out of the loop. And he had heard the rumblings of this latest rumor, his alleged illegitimate child, even before he'd seen his own children discussing it here tonight. He just hoped Nora hadn't heard it yet. He needed to be the one to explain to her.

Reaching a hand up to his wife, he said, "Nora, we need to talk. In private."

"Of course, dear," Nora said, giving Dr. Strickland an apologetic look. The doctor had stopped to say hello before heading back to the hospital.

"Are you feeling ill, sir?" Luke asked, leaning over Wallace.

"I'm fine," Wallace said, his tone curt. "I just want to talk to my wife."

"Then I'll leave you to it," Luke said, concern on his face.

Wallace ignored his hovering doctor, waving him away as Nora wheeled her husband down a hallway to an empty conference room, away from the noise of the party. Wallace craned his neck to make sure the doctor didn't follow them. But Dr. Strickland was headed out the door, Tammy Franklin by his side. Good. He didn't want anyone to overhear this conversation.

"What's wrong, Wallace?" Nora asked, her voice low and unsure.

He hated the fear and pain in her eyes. He took her hands in his and looked up at her. "I love you."

"I love you, too, darling."

"Then I hope you'll understand what I'm about to tell you."

"You're scaring me," Nora said. "Should I get the doctor back in here?"

"No, honey. Just listen." His hands were shaking, but Nora held him steady. "I heard the kids talking—just bits and pieces, but I think I've figured something out."

"What?"

"Another rumor." He shrugged. "I heard things, at the hospital. People whisper when they think I'm asleep. And I've been in the news business a long time. I know the right questions to ask. But I wanted you to hear this from me first." He let out a long shaky sigh. "Before I met you, I was kind of wild. I played around a lot."

Nora's smile was full of tolerance. "I know that, dear."

"But what you don't know is this—I…I was with Betty Owens, before you came along."

Nora stood still, her hands holding on to him. He felt the trembling inside her. "What are you saying, Wallace?"

"Justine might be my child."

"I didn't want to believe that story in the *Observer,* but I'd wondered…"

Nora's whole body slumped, but only for a minute. "It seems we've both been carrying secrets all these years."

"That's why I'm telling you this now," he said, tears biting at his eyes. "I want a clean start, Nora.

I don't want any more secrets between any of us. My family is everything to me, including Jeremy. Especially Jeremy. I don't know if this latest is true, but I heard the kids—I heard Justine's name mentioned, and Betty's name, and I saw the confusion on Tim and Jeremy's faces. I've shamed them yet again. I've shamed you, too."

Nora dropped her hands away. He thought she was going to leave him sitting there, but instead, she hugged him close and whispered. "You married me when I was carrying another man's child, Wallace. How can I even begin to judge what you did before we got married? The shame would be in letting this change things between us. My love for you will never change."

"Are you saying you forgive me, even if this is true?"

"Or course, darling. We've come too far to let the past ruin us now." She straightened, wiped her eyes. "Wallace, you almost died. But we have a second chance. God gave us that. We need to rededicate our lives to the Lord. It's the only way to get through this. We should go see Reverend Abernathy and get right with God again."

"I agree," he said, taking her hand again. "And I promise, I'm going to rededicate myself to you and our marriage, and to our family, too." Then he swallowed hard. "Nora, I have never been unfaithful to you—not since I laid eyes on you, and certainly not since we took our vows."

"That's all I need to hear," she said. Then she kissed his forehead. "It's all going to work out."

Wallace nodded, wiped at his own eyes. "I need to find Jeremy. All this time, I've waited for him to come to me, but I think he did." He lifted his head again. "I think he visited me the other night. I know I heard his voice. He tried to reach out to me, in his own quiet way. But I need to make the next move. I need to make a public acknowledgment and an apology to him. Then I can finally be well again."

Nora smiled. "That sounds like a good plan to me."

Jeremy watched as Ellen Manning smiled and greeted a few of her surprised former coworkers. She was fashionably dressed in a fitted red dress, but she looked tired and harsh, as if she'd had a long, hard day. He was working his way toward her when Gabi came in the door. Relieved to see her, Jeremy waved to Gabi, taking in her pretty burgundy suit and shiny black pumps. She motioned for him to come over. He'd have to talk to Ellen later.

"Hi," he said, taking Gabi by the arm. "I was worried."

"I'm sorry I'm late," she replied, sounding breathless. "I went by the church to make copies for the Christmas Eve church bulletin, but the copier at the church broke down. I couldn't get in touch with anyone to help fix it. I brought the master copy here, hoping I could finish them upstairs, if you don't mind me doing that."

"Of course not," Jeremy said. "I'll take you up there myself."

She shook her head. "No, you don't have to do that. Stay here with your staff and family. I know where the copiers are. I've helped Dawn enough times when she was running behind on meal-delivery night. I'll use the one out by Tim's office, since I know how to run it, if that's okay."

"I don't mind helping," he said. "And besides, we'd get to be alone together."

She smacked his arm, a teasing light in her eyes. "I have to get this done, so I don't need you distracting me."

He ran a hand through his hair. "Will this get us to our romantic dinner quicker?"

"Yes, if you let me get on with it."

"Okay, I do have something to take care of myself. You go on up and I'll meet you there in a few minutes."

"Thanks," she said, hurrying toward the elevator.

Jeremy watched as she explained to the ever-watchful Herman Gordon what she needed. Herman bobbed his head and helped her onto the elevator, then hurried back to his station by the food table.

Jeremy turned his attention back to Ellen. She was talking to the head of advertising and sipping a cup of punch. She glanced around, obviously nervous by the way her hands fluttered as she almost spilled her punch. Deciding it was now or never, he started toward her.

"Jeremy?"

He turned to find his father right behind him. "Hello," he said, noticing Wallace's animated expression. "Are you all right?"

"I'm doing great, son," Wallace said as he wheeled his chair closer. He reached out a hand. Jeremy took that hand, and was surprised to feel the strength as Wallace squeezed his fingers. "We have a lot to talk about, but first, could you get everyone's attention? I need to say a few words."

"Of course," Jeremy said, wondering what was going on. He had yet to have a real conversation with his father. Maybe he should just give up on that. And on confronting Ellen Manning, too, for now. He didn't want to upset his parents or ruin everyone's good cheer. Longing to sneak away with Gabi, Jeremy was torn between duty and need.

But Wallace seemed to have other ideas. He looked impatient and eager. "Jeremy, please?"

Jeremy found a glass and a knife and standing on a low sturdy coffee table, tapped the knife against the crystal to get everyone's attention. A hush fell over the crowd as they saw father and son together for the first time in months.

"Thank you," Jeremy said, forcing a cheery smile. "I'm so glad you're all enjoying the party." Then he hopped down off the table and turned to Wallace. "My father wants to talk to us."

Wallace waited as everyone settled and stilled, his expression unreadable. Jeremy held his breath, then glanced toward his mother. Nora looked excited, but frail and drained. Her eyes were red-rimmed. What was his father up to now? Jeremy didn't want another confrontation. He only wanted a reconciliation. But maybe he had waited too late for that to happen.

Chapter Fifteen

The room was so silent, Jeremy thought he could hear the dry needles falling off the blue spruce Christmas tree. Everyone waited to hear what Wallace had to say.

Wishing Gabi were here, Jeremy watched as his mother put an encouraging hand on Wallace's shoulder. "Go ahead, dear."

Wallace cleared his throat, then looked over at Jeremy.

"Son, I've done some bad things in my time, but the way I treated you when I got sick is probably the worst." He stopped, gathered himself through a deep breath. "So I just want to say here in front of everyone we know and love, that I love you, Jeremy, and I will always consider you my son. My firstborn son. And I hope that you can forgive me."

Wallace lowered his head. Jeremy stood shocked and silent for a minute, then he glanced around. Tim, standing with a teary-eyed Dawn, sent him an encouraging look. Heather and Amy, nearby with Ethan and Bryan, did the same. Chris moved with a policeman's stealth to Jeremy's side, Melissa not far behind. In a matter of seconds, his family had surrounded him, holding him enclosed in a tightly bound circle.

Jeremy swallowed his shame and his pain, seeing everyone he loved right here. Everyone but one person. In that moment, everything suddenly became as clear as a starry winter night in Jeremy's mind. He loved Gabi, and now that he finally felt like part of this family again, he no longer needed to be a part of Hamilton Media empire in order to feel as if he belonged. He also felt true forgiveness in his heart for his father. All the things he'd feared and dreaded over the last few months seemed to melt away, like snow turning into a river, as he stood there. He felt reborn, new, free. And he couldn't wait to begin all over again. With Gabi.

"Son?" Wallace asked, reaching out a hand to Jeremy. "Do you accept my apology?"

Jeremy bent down beside his father's wheelchair, his hand holding on to Wallace. "I do. I do, Father. I forgive you, but there is nothing to forgive. It's over now. I'm home. And I think I'm the one who should be asking for forgiveness." Then he hugged his father close, tears brimming in his eyes. Wallace returned the hug, his hands holding on to Jeremy's back. Jeremy felt his mother's hand on his shoulder, too. He glanced up at her, gave her a watery smile. "I love you both."

"We love you, too," Nora said. "We love all of our children and everyone who works so hard for Hamilton Media."

Wallace held up a hand. "And that's why I'm going to retire and let my children run this place. My only desire for the future is to take my wife on a long honeymoon cruise around the world."

Nora gasped, then grinned like a schoolgirl. "I'd love that, darling, as long as your doctors approve, of course."

Everyone started laughing and talking, and as Jeremy stood again, he saw he wasn't the only one shedding joyful tears. The whole room seemed alive with a new hope, a new radiance. He wanted to find Gabi and tell her what had happened.

Wallace touched his arm. "I'd like to talk to you in private, if you don't mind."

Jeremy nodded, hiding his reluctance, and wheeled his father's chair into the conference room. For a minute, they were silent, Jeremy leaning against the table, Wallace staring up at him.

Finally, Wallace spoke. "Are you sure about this, son?"

"What do you mean?"

Wallace chuckled, reminding Jeremy of the father he'd always known. "It's hard, being face to face at last. Are you sure you're ready to come back?"

Jeremy thought about that for a minute before responding. "I'm sure that I love you and Mom, and I'm sure that things will be fine between us."

"But?"

Jeremy turned to stare out into the night. The street lamps illuminated the sparkling Christmas decorations gracing the streets of Davis Landing. The night looked perfect, like a Christmas card.

But that same old restlessness gnawed at Jeremy. "But…I think I'd like to branch out, maybe start a new project."

"You mean, leave Hamilton Media?"

Jeremy turned back, his hands in the pockets of his corduroy trousers. "Not necessarily, sir. I was thinking more along the lines of starting a new magazine."

"That sounds like a challenge," Wallace said, his voice strong with excitement. "Tell me more."

Jeremy sank back against the table. "It was something Gabi said—"

"Gabi? Ah, the new woman in your life."

"Yes, sir. She told me I might have to reinvent myself, in order to find myself." He fingered a copy of yesterday's edition of the paper lying on the table. And thought, that was it, that was what was making him restless. He didn't want yesterday's edition. He wanted a new beginning. "I think I might like to start a Christian lifestyle magazine, something that will cover the entire southeastern part of the country. Gabi mentioned a need for such a magazine, and that's kind of stuck with me."

"She sounds like a very wise woman."

"She is, in her own quiet way."

"You're in love?"

Jeremy nodded. "Yes, I am."

Wallace gave him a knowing smile. "Then, I'd say go after the new venture, and go and get that woman."

Jeremy stood, raked a hand down his face. "I've been trying to do that all night."

Wallace chuckled again. "Well, don't let me hold you up. I need to find my wife, anyway."

Jeremy wheeled his father out of the room and back into the party, which was even livelier now. Thanking his father, and giving his mother a good hug, he headed toward the elevator.

Only to be stopped by Ellen Manning.

"Jeremy, I'm so glad I caught you," the blonde said, her smile practiced and precise.

Jeremy longed to keep walking, but he needed to clear up this last little bit of business from the past before he could find that new beginning. "Ellen, actually, I wanted to talk to you, too. How are things at the *Observer?*"

Shock registered on her pretty face. "Uh, okay, I guess. I miss my job here, but hey, I've got bills to pay."

Jeremy decided to be direct. "What made you decide to go to work for the competition, anyway?"

She stepped back, her hands shaking as she touched them to her gold necklace. "I...I needed a change."

He didn't buy that. "C'mon, Ellen, you were good at your job with the magazine here. You didn't even give notice. Something must have triggered this."

She glanced around, her expression worried. Jeremy could see the fear in her eyes. What was she hiding? Or better yet, who was she protecting? Finally, she looked back at him, a new determination in her blue eyes. "I felt underappreciated here, Jeremy. I thought I'd be out of Davis Landing by now and it wouldn't matter."

"But instead, you were forced to stay here and to take the first job that came along. I have to wonder why."

"You don't need to worry about that," she said, her bravado covering her obvious unease. "Hey, I've got an idea. Why don't we blow this party and go out for a nice drink, just the two of us?"

Jeremy's antenna went up. Ellen wasn't a very good actress. "Ellen, it's me, Jeremy. Remember, you used to come to me with your problems. If you're in some kind of trouble—"

"I'm fine," she said, backing away. "You can't blame a girl for trying to win back an old friend, now can you?"

"No, but if you need to talk, we can do it right here, upstairs, in private."

"No," she shouted, causing several people nearby to look up. "No," she said again, this time on a low whisper. "I'm sorry, Jeremy. I need to go." Then she touched a manicured hand to his arm. "I really am so sorry."

With that, she rushed past him and headed for the door, pushing at people as she went.

Something was definitely not right with her, Jeremy decided. And that something probably had a lot to do with all the problems his family had been dealing with lately. Had Ellen deliberately been feeding information to reporters at the *Observer?*

It seemed that way, but he still couldn't figure out what purpose it would serve.

"What happened there?" Tim asked, shaking Jeremy out of his fog.

"She knows something," Jeremy said. "I think she's probably the one who's been leaking things to the press about us. It's the obvious answer, except we never gave her any cause to do so." Ellen's being involved was too *obvious*. There had to be more to this.

Tim shrugged. "Sometimes people don't need a reason. She certainly knew a lot about our comings and goings, after working here for so long. It looks pretty clear now. I don't know why we didn't think of her sooner."

Jeremy needed to understand why he still felt unsure, though. "It just doesn't make sense, but I think it might finally be over. I intend to question her again, and get some answers once and for all. I think Ellen came here tonight to confess to us."

"But she chickened out?"

"Yes. I scared her enough, though, that I think it's finally going to end. But I'd still like to hear her side of this."

Tim looked toward the door. "Should we press charges?"

Jeremy would like nothing more, but it didn't seem feasible. "Why? Most of it was true, after all. It caused us embarrassment, but…we're over that now."

"And stronger for it," Tim said. "Maybe we should reinforce that by warning Ellen to back off."

"I can do that," Jeremy said. "First thing tomorrow morning. That is, if I can find her."

Tim lifted his brows. "Well, make sure she understands we mean business. This has gone on long enough."

Jeremy gave him a tired smile. "I'm going to find Gabi right now. I've been trying all night and I really need to see her."

Tim grinned, then punched the elevator button. "I'll make sure you don't get interrupted."

"I'm very sorry for the interruption," the man said as he ushered Gabi into Tim's office.

Gabi's heart pumped so hard she could feel it going bump, bump against her ribcage. She recognized the man, but tried to ignore the big pistol he had aimed at her. "What do you want?"

He chuckled, the sound of his harsh laughter sending shock waves down Gabi's spine. She was alone on the third floor of Hamilton Media with a man who looked and acted very desperate and dangerous. How would anyone find her? Even if she screamed for help, no one would hear her over the jazzy holiday tunes playing downstairs. She just hoped Jeremy would get impatient and come upstairs to check on her. For once, she wouldn't mind his impatience so much. But then, if he did come up here, something might happen to him, too.

"I want what is mine," the man said, waving the gun toward a file cabinet. "And just your luck, sweetheart, you get to help me find it."

"I've seen you before," she said, trying to buy time. "At the hospital." She also remembered him coming out of Betty's that day she'd had lunch with Jeremy and Dawn. She shuddered again. "You've been watching me, haven't you?"

He nodded. "Very observant. I had business at the hospital. But I did notice you, yeah, after you started running with the uptown crowd."

Gabi heard the sarcasm in his tone and wondered what sort of business. "You always stared at me."

He was staring now, in a way that gave her the creeps. Praying that Jeremy would come looking for her, she eased back against a chair. She had to do something soon, or this madman might hurt someone besides her.

"I was watching," he admitted. "You and Jeremy have a thing going on, don't you?"

"That's none of your business."

"I made it my business." He glanced around the elegant office. "I used to work here, so I know a lot about all the Hamiltons. But I'd like to know more."

Gabi swallowed some of her fear, willing herself to stay calm. She glanced toward the door, wondering if she could make a run for it. But then, she'd been trying to find a way out of this from the moment she'd found this man going through a drawer in Dawn's desk just outside the office. Thinking he was an employee, she'd greeted him with a smile. Then he'd turned around, his gun aimed at her, and forced her to come in here.

"Why…why did you quit?" she asked. She wondered why he was back and what could be so important that he'd risk being caught. "I'm sure if you just talk to Jeremy—"

"Talking won't work." He held the gun on her while he rummaged through the desk. "Let's just say your darling Jeremy didn't understand me. He wouldn't pay me what I was worth, so I had to take matters into my own hands. He fired me, sent me packing with all this brotherly concern. Now I'm going to get even once and for all."

"Jeremy is a good man. Maybe he wanted to spare you any more embarrassment."

"Yeah, right. Something you need to understand, sweetheart. The Hamiltons are only for Hamiltons. That's the way it works around here. And Jeremy should know that firsthand by now."

Gabi realized he would do anything to get what he wanted. Apparently, he wanted something in this office. "What are you after now?"

He shook his head. "Nothing for you to worry about, but you do present a problem. After we find it, what am I going to do with you?"

"You could let me go."

"Right. And you'd run for Jeremy in a heartbeat. I don't think so."

She watched as he pulled out files with one hand, his gun trained on her with the other. Looking around for a weapon of her own, she saw a bronze rockshaped paper weight on the credenza behind her. If she could just reach it—

The man looked more angry by the minute. His

frown turned to an ugly scowl as he mumbled to himself. "Where did you hide the proof, Jeremy?"

"This is Tim's office now," Gabi said, her mind filling with questions. What kind of proof did this man need?

His head came up as he glanced around, shocked. The split second gave Gabi just enough time to inch toward the credenza. He didn't seem to notice. "Do you know where they keep the family records?"

"No, you know I don't work here. I was just using the copier outside."

He let out a frustrated sigh, then kicked at a chair, giving her enough time to slip the paperweight inside her suit pocket. "Maybe we should just call Jeremy and Tim up here after all. They're probably both in on this."

Fearful that he would hurt Jeremy, Gabi shook her head. "If you're looking for some sort of records, those would probably be down the hall in Jeremy's new office. He took on a new position when he came back." If she could get him back out into the hallway, she might have a chance. "Or maybe across the hallway, in Personnel. Jeremy works closely with that department now."

He slammed a drawer shut. "I just need enough money to get me out of this town. But I need proof, first, to get that money." Then he turned toward the door. "Let's go to Personnel then."

Gabi gasped. "Are you talking about blackmail?"

"C'mon," he said, motioning to her with the gun. He didn't answer her. He waited for her to go ahead of him. "You can show me the records, since you seem to know where they are. And if that doesn't work, well, we'll just take a ride to the hospital. Since you work there, in administration, you can probably show me Wallace Hamilton's medical history."

"No," she said, feeling the heavy paperweight inside her pocket. "I told you, I don't know my way around here, and I can't access patient medical files at the hospital. I work in the billing department."

He shoved her out the door, ignoring her arguments. "There's one last secret I need to verify. The Hamiltons won't want anyone to know this latest. It would be the end of them." He grabbed her by the arm. "And since you were in the wrong place at the wrong time, you will help me."

Gabi's fear tasted bitter and metallic as she gazed up at him. "I won't do anything to hurt Jeremy or his family."

He shoved her, causing her to hit a knee against a filing cabinet. "You'll do whatever I tell you to do."

Gabi braced herself against the metal cabinet, her hand going for the paperweight as she turned around. Seeing her chance, she lunged for him. "I don't think so," she shouted, using all her force to bring the round dark object up against his head.

He looked shocked, then groaned in pain, his hand coming up to his head. Dropping the gun, he fell to the floor at about the same time the elevator doors opened.

"Jeremy!" Gabi screamed his name, so glad to

see him she had to grab the desk to steady herself. "Jeremy, help."

Jeremy took one look at Gabi and the man lying at her feet, kicked the gun across the room far from Curtis, then ran the rest of the way toward her. "What happened?"

"He—he was up here when I came up," she said, her teeth chattering. "He...he was after something."

Jeremy pulled her to him, running a hand over her hair. "Are you all right?"

"I am now," she said. "He has a gun."

Jeremy gently sat her down in Dawn's desk chair, then grabbed the phone. The man at his feet moaned, tried to sit up, but Jeremy pushed him back down with a fist clutching at his shirtfront. "Chris, it's Jeremy. Get upstairs right now. Curtis Resnick just attacked Gabi."

Jeremy watched as Chris circled Curtis's chair. His younger brother was in full cop mode—and not in good-cop mode.

"Want to go over this one more time?" Chris asked, lifting Curtis by the chin. "What were you doing, Curtis?"

Curtis jerked his face away, then let out a groan. "My head hurts. I need a lawyer and a doctor."

"On the way," Chris said, leaning close. "And you're gonna *need* that lawyer. Breaking and entering, assault, attempted blackmail. Captain Driscoll isn't going to be too happy with you. He's on his way, too, by the way."

"Hey, *she* hit *me*," Curtis said, giving Gabi a scowl.

Jeremy joined his brother in front of Resnick. "Only because you were holding a gun on her," he said, his anger so palpable, he wondered how he had managed not to beat Resnick to a pulp.

Gabi, he thought. He turned to where she sat, knowing he'd only held back for her sake. He stood, turning to his brother. "I'll let you handle this, Chris. I need to take Gabi home. You have enough from her for a statement, right?"

Chris gave a nod. "For now. We might need to go over some things later."

Tim came out of his office. "I'll stay here with Chris," he said, his features harsh and all business. "I'd really like to hear what Curtis has to say."

Jeremy urged Gabi out of the chair. "Let's get you out of here."

"My copies," she said, her voice just above a whisper.

Jeremy smiled at that. "Gabi, Dawn will handle that, honey. You're in shock. You don't need to stay here."

She nodded, her eyes never leaving his face. "Jeremy—"

He pulled her inside Tim's office, then held her in his arms, away from the commotion outside. "I'm so sorry, Gabi."

"I'm okay," she said, her hands clinging to his sweater. "It's just that—"

"It's just that he scared you," Jeremy finished, kissing her head. "It's over now."

"But he wanted something," she replied, anxiety clear in her dark eyes. "I think he was planning on blackmailing you. He kept saying he needed proof."

Jeremy let out breath. "I think I know what he was looking for. He's obviously the one who's been leaking all the rumors about my family. The latest one, about my father possibly being Justine Owens Grimes's father, hasn't been substantiated. He probably wanted information about that."

She stared up at him, still in shock. "Is it true?"

"We don't know." He held her close again. "And frankly, I don't care. Right now, I'm only concerned about you."

"The girls," she said, bringing a hand to her mouth.

"I called Angela Hart," he said. "They're fine. She said they can stay with Lauren and Samantha tonight. They're safe."

He felt her begin to shake. "Are you sure?"

"I'm sure, honey. Richard and Melissa went home to check on them. They're all right."

She gave a brief nod, her eyes wide. "Okay."

"Let me take you home."

She didn't argue with him.

Jeremy had her headed toward the door when Tim came barreling in. "You won't believe this," Tim said with a red-faced frown.

"What now?"

Tim shot a glance toward Gabi.

"Go ahead," Jeremy said. "Gabi has a right to hear this, since she's involved, too, now."

Tim looked down at the floor. "They were in it together, Resnick and Ellen Manning. That's why she quit so suddenly. After you let Curtis go, he started sweet-talking Ellen for information. She gave it to him, then he convinced her to quit, too. And now he's more than willing to give up the goods on her. Apparently, they'd planned on leaving Davis Landing together, after Resnick had destroyed our family, of course."

Jeremy stood silent, holding tightly to Gabi's hand. Gabi looked at Tim. "He said he needed proof about one last thing."

Tim nodded. "Yeah, well, he seems to think Justine *is* our half-sister."

"But we had heard that," Jeremy said. "How could that possibly destroy us, since half the town's been talking about it anyway?"

"Yeah, but there's more," Tim retorted. "He thinks Justine was the donor for our father, Jeremy. He says she's the one who gave bone marrow. And that was the information he was hoping to find here tonight. Think about it—Gabi said he'd been snooping around the hospital, too. When he didn't find anything there, he came here." Tim hit a hand on the doorjamb. "That would certainly have made a juicy article in the *Observer*."

Jeremy's gaze locked with his brother's. "We need to warn Mom and Dad. And we have to protect Justine, too."

"I know," Tim said. "Listen, why don't you take Gabi home and let me take care of that. I'll call you later."

"Okay," Jeremy said. "Call a family meeting at the house. I'll meet y'all there later."

Tim held the door for them. Chris stood outside, watching as another policeman took Curtis away. "I sent a patrol to find Ellen," he told his brothers. "I don't know if we can make anything stick, but she *is* an accessory. And a witness, if nothing else. According to Resnick, she came to the party tonight to distract you, Jeremy."

"Those two deserve each other," Jeremy said, watching as Curtis turned at the elevator, a look of pure hatred on his face.

"This isn't over, Jeremy," he shouted, straining against being held.

Jeremy gently put Gabi beside his brother, then stalked to where Resnick stood. Grabbing Curtis by the lapels with white-knuckled fists, Jeremy got right in his face. "I think it is. Because if you ever set foot near me or anyone I love again, I won't be responsible for my actions. You are all out of second chances. Just remember that, Resnick." He pushed a visibly shaken Curtis away.

Then he hurried back to Gabi. "C'mon. I promised you a quiet dinner and I keep my promises, no matter what."

Chapter Sixteen

"He insists, Mom. He wants to do this by himself."

Nora looked from Tim's concerned expression to her husband's stubborn, tight-lipped frown. "Wallace, it's late and we've had enough excitement for one night. Let me take you home now."

Wallace shook his head. "I just need a few minutes, Nora. Heather can take you home if you don't want to wait."

"I'll be glad to," Heather said, as she shot Tim a questioning look. "We all need time to let this soak in. I can't believe Curtis was behind all of this."

"Figures," Wallace retorted, his hands folded over his lap. "I never did trust that man."

"It's over now, darling," Nora said, her words quiet and focused in spite of the pain in her eyes. "I'm so glad Gabi wasn't hurt. Jeremy must be beside himself."

"He took her home," Heather said. "And Dawn's upstairs monitoring things for Tim. We'll have to do some damage control, but with Felicity covering the story I think we'll be okay. We're going to get through this."

Nora placed a hand on Tim's arm. "I appreciate you helping with your father."

"I'm right here," Wallace said, giving all of them a hard-eyed stare. "You don't have to whisper and fuss. I just need to do this. To end all of it, for good."

Tim glanced around at the now-empty lobby of Hamilton Media. Once word had filtered down to the crowd about the situation upstairs, the party had gone from joyful to somber. Most of the group had either gone home, or rushed to their respective stations to get the latest on this interesting story. Ed Bradshaw was hard at work, sending people in all directions to gather background history on Curtis and Ellen. Felicity was already on the lead story, gathering information and facts for the next issue of the *Dispatch*. They'd all agreed they might as well get the jump on the *Observer* and tell their story themselves, just to set the record straight. Tim trusted Felicity to get the story accurate, and that included the final twist of the puzzle. Justine Owens Grimes. They had to protect Justine. They wouldn't divulge her name unless she agreed to let them.

Tim itched to be in on the action upstairs, but felt obligated to help his father with this latest request. Wallace wanted to talk to Betty and Justine. "I'll take him over there, Mother. Go with Heather. We'll be home soon."

Nora touched a hand to Wallace's sleeve. "Are you sure?"

He turned from sullen to gentle. "Yes. I need to thank them. If this is true, I owe Justine my life."

"I understand," Nora said. She straightened as Heather took her by the arm and guided her out of the building.

Tim waited a minute, then pushed his father's wheelchair toward the door. Turning to Herman Gordon, he said, "Don't lock up. I'll be back in a little while."

Herman sent him a salute. "I don't plan on going anywhere until you say so."

Wallace waved a hand to Tim to stop as they entered Betty's. The place was empty since it was very near closing time, and the tinkling bell on the door sounded loud in the silent restaurant. Betty came out of the back, her gaze taking in the two men standing in the doorway.

"Wallace," she said, her tone light in spite of the uncertainty in her eyes. "It's good to see you."

Wallace glanced up at Tim. "Give us a minute, son."

Tim hesitated, then said, "I'll go check on things at the office. I'll be back in a few minutes."

Wallace rolled his chair closer to where Betty stood. "I guess you know why I'm here."

Betty nodded, wiped at the counter. "We heard the sirens, saw them taking Curtis away. Word gets out pretty quickly around here."

"What did you hear?"

"Oh, that Curtis attacked Gabi Valencia when she caught him snooping in the upstairs offices."

Wallace waited as her expression changed. "Why, is there something more?"

Wallace nodded. "Curtis seems to think he had something on us, something he could use against us. It involves you and Justine."

Betty went pale, bringing a hand to her throat. "Oh, Wallace."

"Is it true?" he asked, without preamble. If he'd learned anything in the last few months, it was to get to the point, then get on with life.

Betty sank down on a chair next to him, her eyes on the salt and pepper shakers sitting on the table. "Justine doesn't want to know if you're her father or not. She considers Harold to be her father. I'd like to leave it that way."

Wallace looked down at his hands. "And yet, she was willing to donate her bone marrow to me."

Betty let out a sigh, glanced back toward the kitchen. "Yes. She never hesitated on that part. But she didn't want anyone to find out. I'm so sorry, Wallace."

Wallace let out a grunt. "I'm the one who came to apologize, Betty. I wasn't a very nice man back then. I did you wrong. It's no wonder you never told me the truth."

Betty tidied up the plastic daisies centered on the checkered tablecloth. "I met Harold and things just worked out. There was no need to bother you. You had Nora, I had Harold. I think it all worked out the way it was meant to work out."

Wallace brought his head up then. "Justine saved my life. How can I ever repay you or her for that?"

Betty took one of his hands in hers. "By being a good man, Wallace. By loving your family, by doing what you've always done. You are a part of this community. We all need you around. Just... appreciate what you have."

He chuckled, but the prick of tears pierced at his eyes. "I am one very blessed man. Nora knows everything and she's willing to stand by me. Now you and Justine—you've given so much to me. After all I've done—"

"We're even now," Betty said. "Let's just let it go at that."

He patted her hand. "If you ever need anything—"

Then he heard footsteps in the kitchen and looked up to find Justine staring at him from the door. "I'm glad you're doing okay," she said, hanging back, a look of resolve on her face.

Wallace reached out his arms. "I need to thank you."

Justine rushed to him and hugged him close. "Take care of yourself."

"I aim to do that," Wallace said. "And you two do the same."

Justine stood, her hand on his shoulder. "We're going to be just fine."

Wallace believed that. Betty was a strong, proud woman. And so was her daughter. He turned the wheelchair around and slowly pushed toward the door.

Tim found him sitting at the window, looking out into the night. "Ready?" he asked.

"I am," Wallace said.

Tim turned to Betty and Justine. They stood with their arms locked, watching Tim and Wallace. He gave Justine a direct look, which she returned, her eyes dark with emotion as an unspoken message of thanks and forgiveness passed between them. Then she turned and went back into the kitchen, and Tim turned to take his father home.

The little house seemed so empty.

Gabi locked the door behind them, then turned back to face Jeremy. "Thanks for bringing me home."

He took her coat, then guided her to the sofa in the small, cozy den. Without a word, he hung her coat on the rack by the door, turned on a nearby lamp, then headed into the kitchen. She sat staring at the twinkling lights on the Christmas tree, thinking she really needed to buy that sweater Roni had seen at Engel's the other day. That was one last gift she needed to get. And maybe a necklace for Talia. Yes, Talia loved dainty jewelry.

Just keep thinking mundane thoughts, she told herself. Keep the fear, the panic away. She sat with her arms held tightly around her stomach, the familiar sounds coming from the kitchen bringing her comfort. She heard the cabinet door slapping shut, heard water running, then the ping of the microwave buzzer. She wasn't alone.

"Here," Jeremy said, coming to sit by her.

The hot tea steamed a soft mist of cinnamon

and mint toward her nostrils as she took the cup. "Thank you." She held the cup in both hands for just a minute, until Jeremy took it from her.

"You're shaking," he said. He moved toward her, pulling her close as he settled on the sofa beside her. "I'm so sorry this happened to you. I should have gone upstairs with you."

"You had no way of knowing he'd be there," she said, the warmth of his arms giving her strength. "Besides, I'm all right, honestly. Just a little jittery."

Jeremy pulled back, then lifted her chin around toward him. He gave her a warm kiss, holding her close as if he could will her to relax and forget the horror of being held at gunpoint. Gabi sank against him, then lifted her head so she could see his face. "I need to tell you something."

"Okay." He reached for her tea. "Drink some of this first."

She took a sip, letting the warm liquid burn a path down to her stomach. "That's good."

He put the cup back down. "What's wrong?"

"Nothing," she said through a smile. "Nothing, all things considered."

He brushed a strand of hair away from her cheek. "You're safe now."

She believed him. Somehow, she knew this man would always keep her safe. "I need you to understand," she began, her heart stepping up its pace, "about Octavio."

"What about him?" His question was soft and re-assuring.

"He committed suicide, Jeremy."

Jeremy tugged back to stare over at her, shock evident on his face. "You never told me—"

"I didn't want you to know. I asked Dawn to keep it quiet, too."

"But why?"

"I was ashamed," she said, sinking back on the sofa. "I blamed myself. I still blame myself."

Jeremy angled around to look at her. "But why? I mean, what happened?"

"He lost his job at one of the local factories. It was hard on him, being laid off like that, having to sit around and do nothing. He didn't handle it very well, and I just kept on working and worrying, hoping he'd pull out of it. But he sank into a deep depression, and he resented me because I had a job. He couldn't deal with me being the breadwinner when he could only sit here and worry every day. Even with unemployment checks coming in, he still suffered. He was the kind of man who had to have work. He prided himself on being able to take care of his family. He needed something to prove himself." She shifted, brought her hands together. "I tried to get him to go to a doctor, but Octavio had too much pride for that. In the end, he just gave up."

"I'm so sorry," Jeremy said, bringing her back into his arms. "No wonder you were so afraid of getting close to me." He leaned his head against hers, his chin brushing her forehead. "I was in a bad way when I got back home."

She bobbed her head. "It scared me. I thought,

'not again.' I didn't want to have to deal with that again."

"You compared me to him?"

"I did. But now I can see that was so wrong. You are so very different from him."

"I thought you were still mourning him, still in love with him."

"I do still love him, but…that didn't stop my feelings for you. And I felt so guilty."

"I kept pushing you, thinking I could make you forget him."

She sighed, snuggled into his arms. "You were stubborn. You *are* stubborn."

"I have my pride, too," he said, and she could feel his smile. "I wanted you to have feelings for me."

"You do have that same sense of pride that he had. But you also have an inner strength that has helped you through the worst. I think I can deal with you now, especially after tonight. I almost lost the chance ever to tell you all of this. I almost lost the chance to be happy again."

She felt his shudder. "You risked your life. If anything had happened to you, Gabi—"

"I'm okay," she said, turning to touch his face. "I just needed you to understand why I was so afraid of…loving you."

"Do you?" he asked, his eyes going wide with hope and longing. "Do you love me?"

"I'm pretty sure I do, *sì*. I realized that tonight, when that man held that gun to my head. I thought about all my doubts and fears and realized I might not have the chance to show you how much I cared about you. That scared me much more than loving you ever could. I thought about my children and how they needed a father, and I thought about how I needed you in my life. And I wondered what I'd been so afraid of."

"I'm here," he said, kissing her again. "I'm here, Gabi. I want to make this work. You don't have to be afraid. I love you."

"I love you, too," she said. "But…we have to be sure. The girls are so fragile—"

"I understand. The girls have to approve of me."

"I think they will. I believe they just need time."

"I'll show them, Gabi. I'll show them I can keep a promise."

She tugged him close. "I believe you."

He laughed then, his face bright with joy. "I didn't get to tell you *my* news."

"What?"

"My father and I mended our fences tonight at the party."

"You did? Oh, that's wonderful. I hate that I missed it."

He laughed. "It was pretty incredible. He asked me to forgive him, right there in front of everyone."

"You needed that, Jeremy."

"I know. I didn't realize how much until he did it. We had a good talk. I told him about the new magazine."

"*Our* magazine?" she asked, awe brightening her eyes.

"Yes, that magazine. I decided to take your advice."

She smiled over at him. "You are definitely re-inventing yourself, being with me, starting a new magazine."

"Yes, and I've never felt more sure about anything in my life." He held her close for a minute, then said, "Now about that candlelight dinner—"

"I have candles and I have my mother's home-made tamales," she said, grinning. "How does that sound?"

"Wonderful." He kissed her again, then got up. "You stay right there. I'll heat up the tamales and bring the candles close."

"Okay," she said. She watched as he moved around her tiny kitchen, his presence filling it as if he belonged there. But then, he was the kind of man who could belong just about anywhere. And to Gabi, he looked just right, being here with her.

"Thank You, God," she whispered.

She couldn't have asked for a more perfect Christmas gift.

Epilogue

Christmas Day

"Thanks again for the earrings," Gabi told Jeremy as they stood by the Christmas tree at the Hamilton mansion. "I do love them."

"You're welcome." He gave her a quick kiss, making her feel as if she were the only person in the crowded family room. "I had to get something to match that pretty necklace the girls picked out for you."

She fingered the dainty, glittering diamond necklace looped around her neck. "Oh, you mean the one that only cost, let's see, about twenty dollars?"

"Yes, that would be the one."

She shook her head, grinning up at him. "I should make you return it, but I've grown attached to it already. And the girls would be so disappointed. You should have seen their eyes when I opened it first thing this morning."

"Well, I'm glad you like it. It looks good on you, especially with that red dress you're wearing."

"I've grown attached to you, too," she said, whispering the words in his ear.

"I like the sound of that."

Gabi's heart sang with happiness. "This is so nice, being here for Christmas dinner with your family."

Jeremy lowered his head, leaning in close. "I got an early-morning call from my grandparents in Florida. Chester himself called, to say my grandmother misses me and wants me to come and visit again."

Gabi put a hand to her mouth. "Which means so does he, probably."

"That's what I'm hoping." He tugged her into his arms as they surveyed the crowded room. "Everyone is here. I'm glad your parents allowed me to bring you and the girls."

Her sigh was full of contentment. "Well, we did have our big dinner with them last night, right after the church service."

"And we'll go back by there tonight, just to keep everyone happy." Then he frowned. "Even though I'm still not sure I'm welcome there."

"Afraid my brothers are going to beat you up?"

"Absolutely."

He pulled her around so quickly, she had to catch her breath. "Jeremy?"

"I'm planning on settling things with your brothers. I'm going to ask their permission, and your father's too, to marry you. How do you think they'll feel about that?"

Gabi's heart felt as if it might burst out of her chest. "Are you serious?"

"Extremely." He nuzzled her ear. "I want to make you my wife. Will you marry me, Gabi?"

"I thought we agreed to take this slow."

"I've been patient. I waited three whole days." He gave her a pleading look. "And...we can have a long engagement. I just need to know that you'll consider it."

"I...uh...thought we were supposed to clear things like this with the girls."

"I did, and they've already given me their consent."

She stepped back, surprise registering on her face as she heard a soft giggle from Talia. "So does everyone but me know about this?"

"Yes!" came the reply from several people who'd been standing nearby.

Dawn laughed and clapped, then kissed Tim. He lifted his tea glass to Jeremy. Ethan snapped a picture, while Heather smiled and wiped at her eyes. Chris and Felicity grinned at them from their perch by the fireplace. Bryan and Amy shouted "Hurray" in unison while Bryan's son Dylan ran by, chasing Talia. And Melissa sat holding Richard's hand, her eyes glowing with love and appreciation.

"Welcome back," she called to Jeremy. "And welcome to the family Gabi."

Gabi's gaze moved from Jeremy's expectant face to all those of the people she'd come to know and love in this room. Her eyes touched on Nora's and held. Nora nodded her approval, tears of happiness streaming down her face. Then Gabi watched as Nora tugged at her husband's sleeve.

Wallace stepped forward, walking slowly toward Jeremy and Gabi. "I'd like to say something," he said, his voice rising strong and sure above the din of whispers and laughter. "First of all, congratulations, Jeremy. Gabi, we're honored to have you and the girls as a part of our family." The room hushed as Wallace handed Jeremy a small black velvet box. "But don't you need a ring?"

Jeremy looked surprised, then shrugged sheepishly. "All the stores are closed."

"That is no excuse," Wallace said, his tone good-natured. "Here, take this one."

Jeremy opened the box to reveal a shining solitaire diamond. "Isn't this—"

"It was my first ring," Nora said, smiling. "Your father gave me a new one for Christmas." She waved her left hand, revealing a giant cluster of diamonds. Then she came over and took Gabi's hand in hers. "If you don't want it—"

"It's beautiful," Gabi said, her throat tight, "but I don't think I should be the one—"

"Nonsense," Wallace said, his gaze landing on Jeremy. "You are going to be the wife of my first-born. That means you deserve this ring. And don't worry, she has plenty of others to share with all of her daughters and daughters-in-law."

That brought a round of laughter. Then Gabi felt a tug at her side. Roni and Talia were standing there, their faces full of expectation.

"Try it on, Mama," Talia said.

Gabi looked down at Roni. "Should I, Veronica?"

Roni looked from Gabi to Jeremy and back. "I think so, Mama." Then she grinned and rushed to Jeremy's side. He hugged her close, then took the ring out of the box.

Gabi waited as he placed it on her finger. "It fits," she said, tears streaming down her face. "It fits."

"And so do you," Jeremy said, his whisper soft against her skin. "Now if I can just survive your brothers—"

"I'll handle them," Gabi announced.

Jeremy took that as a yes, pulling her into his arms for another kiss.

Everyone started laughing and talking again. Vera Mae came to the door, her arms on her hips. "Y'all gonna chatter all afternoon or are you gonna get in here and eat this meal we been preparing for days?"

"I'm hungry," Chris said, tugging Felicity toward the dining room. "I think I smell potato rolls."

"Me, too," Tim said, following, his hand on Dawn's back. "I get a drumstick."

In a matter of minutes, everyone was settled around the big table, with a smaller table for the children nearby.

"Wallace, will you say grace?" Nora asked, her eyes full of love and contentment.

"I'd be honored," Wallace said. "I want to tell the Lord how thankful I am for all of my many blessings." He looked from one face to the next, his heart filling with a newfound peace and joy. "I've learned a lot of things over the past few months, the most important being that there is nothing stronger than a family's love."

With that, he gave thanks to God, his hand clasped in Nora's.

"Amen," came the chorus when he was finished.

Wallace sat back and enjoyed being with his family again. He looked over at Jeremy and sent him a hesitant smile. His son's serious gaze held his for a minute, then Jeremy grinned. This truly was a Christmas homecoming, for all of them.

* * * * *

HEARTWARMING INSPIRATIONAL ROMANCE

Contemporary,
inspirational romances
with Christian characters
facing the challenges
of life and love
in today's world.

**AVAILABLE IN REGULAR
AND LARGER-PRINT FORMATS.**

For exciting stories that reflect traditional values,
visit:
www.ReaderService.com

Love Inspired®
SUSPENSE
RIVETING INSPIRATIONAL ROMANCE

Watch for our series of edge-
of-your-seat suspense novels.
These contemporary tales
of intrigue and romance
feature Christian characters
facing challenges to their faith...
and their lives!

AVAILABLE IN REGULAR
& LARGER-PRINT FORMATS

For exciting stories that reflect traditional values,
visit:
www.ReaderService.com